C0-DXB-825

Copyright © 2023 A[illegible]nna and AJ Mullican

All rights reserved.

The characters and events portrayed in this book are fictitious. Any similarity to real persons, living or dead, is coincidental and not intended by the authors.

No part of this book may be reproduced, or stored in a retrieval system, or transmitted in any form or by any means, electronic, mechanical, photocopying, recording, or otherwise, without express written permission of the publishers.

Cover design by: GetCovers

Dedication

This is dedicated to the music that's within all of us, to the songs our souls play. It's dedicated to all those weird little stories mulling around inside, begging for release into the wild. It's dedicated to that musical part within each and every one of us, that orchestra of creativity.

Prologue

"Are you coming with or not, Cassandra?" a voice yells out to me. The words drip with irritation, but I can't force myself to care. I'm tired and can't make up my mind; all I want to do is put on some music and take a nap. That's how I like spending most of my days: away from the world, drifting in my own space.

There are five of us on this trip. We hiked for over two hours before finding the perfect spot to pitch our tents, and now that camp is set up, everyone wants to head down to the lake for a swim before evening sets in. I'm beyond exhausted from the walk and am ready to kick back and relax. It seems, however, that everyone has something else in mind for me.

"Well, are you coming or not?" This time the voice sounds more than just irritated. It makes me feel like I can't say no even though I just want to stay here.

"Yeah, I guess," I reply. I grab a towel and my iPod as I walk towards the four others who stare at me impatiently.

I think I'd be totally lost without my iPod.

"It's about time!" I hear someone remark under their breath. "I was about ready to hog-tie you and drag you to the lake myself."

Everyone's chatting back and forth; they're excited to be spending a week in the woods together before we enter our final year of high school. I listen to stories from the past year, words spilling out of their mouths, everyone trying to speak over the other. It's almost too much to listen to. The overlapping conversations begin to run together, and I have a hard time paying attention to anything that is being said.

Unlike them, I long to be home. In the comfort of my room. Reading a book, listening to the radio, sleeping. My anxiety always kicks in when I go on trips. I hate the way it makes me feel, but when they invited me, my parents overheard the conversation and decided on their own that it would be good for me to get out of the house and have fun with friends. I tried to argue with them about it and gave them several reasons why I thought I should stay home. They refused to listen.

I continue to follow everyone down the small winding path, and we finally come to a clearing where the lake is. There's a small sandy beach right after the trees. The water is a sparkling blue that reflects the brightness of the sun. The tree branches sway from a light breeze that blows across the water. I close my eyes and turn my face to the sky, listening to the rustling sound.

Before I can even think, everyone is diving in, splashing around in the water and shouting at each other. They carry on like children. I lay a towel on the sand and sit down.

I've never been a fan of lakes, ponds, or rivers. Any source of water other than my bathtub gives me the creeps. Just the thought of swimming with other creatures, forcing yourself into their home, never knowing what lurks just below the surface ... I shiver thinking about all the little slimy creatures that live in that water.

"Are you really going to sit there?" Adam calls to me. "You could've just stayed at the campsite if you didn't want to swim."

"Maybe I'll get in in a few," I reply. I put my headphones on and crank my music so I'm no longer able to hear them. I lay back, close my eyes, and revel in the heat of the sun kissing my skin. I let the music soothe me, easing my anxiety of being away from the safety of my home. I drift away and let the rhythms clear the cluttered thoughts in my head. Just as I'm close to freeing my mind from the torment and thoughts, an uneasiness comes over me. Something is staring at me. I know it. And it's closing in on me.

I open my eyes slowly, fearful of what's there. The sun blinds me, and I can't see. Tiny black dots dance across my eyes, and something grabs my ankle. It begins pulling me, dragging me across the sand. I scream and kick frantically trying to escape. I yell for the others to help me as I fight to free myself.

My headphones slide off my head, and laughter assails me. My vision clears, the black dots fade into the background, and Adam stands above me, a huge smile on his face. I kick him in the shin and stand up. I feel disgusted by the cruel joke that has been played on me. He dances around holding his leg and curses me under his breath.

I pick up my towel and storm off towards our campsite. As irritated as I am by the jerk, I'm more frustrated that I let it get to me. Halfway down the path, the trees seem to close in around me. I feel as though I'm suffocating. Panic sets in. I breathe deeply, slowly counting to take my mind off of everything.

"Hey, don't be mad," Adam says as he trots up behind me. "I was just having a little fun with you."

"Yeah, well, you're a jerk."

Just then the others walk up, still giggling about the prank. The smiles on their faces burn me, and I want to punch them all. I just shake my head and continue walking, wanting to leave them behind and escape the embarrassment.

"You should've seen the look on your face." Amanda chuckles. "It was classic. I wish I had been recording that!"

Amanda was my best friend, up until this point. I am now reevaluating our friendship, trying to figure out why I need her as a friend. We normally spend all of our time together, have almost all of our classes together. Our friendship always worked out great because she loved to hear herself talk, and I was good at listening.

As we approach our camp, we all stop and gape at the sight of it. Two of the tents are ripped to shreds, and the items that were once inside lie in piles around the site. It looks as if a bear has come through and decided to take advantage of us being away.

"Well, that's just great!" Kayley shouts as she begins to gather her clothes, which are strewn everywhere. A shorter redhead, Kayla followed our group around until we took her in. "Just look at this; half of my clothes are ruined. What am I supposed to do now?"

"Look, we still have two good tents. Let's just clean up the mess and crash for the night. Tomorrow we'll take off. There's no point leaving now because we'll never make it back to the car before dark," Carl answers.

I roll my eyes. "That's not a good idea. What if it comes back? We don't even know what did this. I'm ready to go home—now."

I go into my undamaged tent and start packing what little I had unpacked before we left for the beach. I refuse to be stuck in the middle of nowhere with something lurking in the woods. It could be out there right now, watching us. Waiting for the perfect moment ...

"Pump the breaks, Cass," Kayley says as she comes into the tent. "He's right, you know. We'll never make it back to the car before it gets dark. If we can't see where we're going, we'll get lost. It's better to stay together here for the night and leave in the morning."

I grunt something about them being right but continue to pack my items. At first light I'm out of here, with or without them. I'm not going to stick around any longer than I have to. Outside the tent, the others pick up their stuff while discussing who is sleeping where for the night. Bags loaded, I exit the tent and walk smack into a heated argument.

"Don't be stupid," Amanda says. "Girls in one tent, boys in the other. Adam, why don't you be useful for once and build a fire. Maybe that will keep away whatever it is that ruined our campsite."

Adam looks at Carl. "I'm not doing this by myself." He grins. Carl agrees to go with and gather wood for the fire. They wander around the perimeter of the camp gathering up what timber they can find, trying to stay close to the campsite so us girls won't be left alone. They take turns, one keeping watch as the other picks up whatever might burn.

After the fire is going, everyone seems to settle down and relax except for me. My mind envisions vicious creatures peering through the trees at us, licking their lips, waiting for the perfect chance to jump out and devour us. My eyes dart from one area to another, keeping watch.

One of the guys heats up some stew and passes it around, making sure everyone eats before bed. I turn down the food and stare into the flames, still wondering what tore up our campsite. It had to be a bear, right? Hungry and looking for some food. The thought makes me nauseous.

A few hours have passed, and it's

pitch-black outside. The fire has almost died out, and the little red embers are the only light available. Adam gets up and takes out his phone, using the light of the screen as a flashlight. "I'm going to get a few more pieces of wood to see if we can get this fire going again," he says as he looks at me. "Tell the others I'll be right back." The sarcasm in his voice is evident. Everyone else has already fallen asleep.

"You shouldn't go alone," I say as I follow after him. "We should stay in groups just in case something happens."

It's so dark that even the light from his phone has a hard time cutting through the blackness. I stumble over unknown objects trying to keep up with him. My mind starts playing tricks on me. I hear footsteps following us, close behind. I ask Adam if he can hear anything or if I'm imagining it, and he just ignores me. I'm losing it for sure.

He piles several pieces of wood into my arms and picks up some logs to carry as well. We head back to the others. I'm a little jealous that everyone else was comfortable enough to fall asleep. My anxiety and fears refuse to let me close my eyes. I find it hard to breathe when my mind takes over and makes everything seem bigger than it is

We approach our destination, and Adam begins to place the new logs onto the red embers. Knowing it isn't going to ignite on its own, he takes out the lighter fluid and covers the pit, tossing a match into the center. In an instant, the fire lights up the darkness instantly, and we back away from the gory site before us, our eyes wide. From the look on his face, he's just as terrified as I am by what the firelight reveals.

Our friends lie on the ground, blood pooling around each of their bodies. Limbs lying unmoving in the dirt. Their eyes are open but blank, glaring lifelessly up at the night sky. There are chunks of skin torn from their bodies. I shiver at the sight, tears welling up in my eyes. My whole body is shaking, and I can't speak. Adam stands still, a look of horror on his face.

"We were only gone for, like, ten minutes," Adam whispers. "What could have done this in that little bit of time?" His face is pale white, and I can tell he is scared. "We didn't even hear anything. It had to have happened really fast, or there is more than one of them."

My mind runs away with the whats and whys of everything. A serial killer, a wild animal, something not of this world has swooped in and taken our friends away from us. I don't want to stay around and find out what it was.

"I want to leave now," I say in a panic. "Whatever it is, it's still out there, and I'm sure it will be back. Let's just go."

A rustling in the leaves catches both of our attention, and we look off into the black nothingness of the woods that lie before us. We fall silent to listen. I'm trying to see how close it is, trying to see something other than the dark, but there's nothing. Just the sound of the leaves moving and sticks breaking in the distance.

"I want to go home." Barely audible

words fall from my mouth. I take a few steps back, tripping over something, and I fall to the ground. Adam bends down to help me up, and the unknown grabs him from behind. Its eyes glow white, and at first that's all I can see. An evil radiating white light coming from sunken eye sockets. And then it grins at me, jagged teeth showing.

It drags Adam away into the tree line. Just as quickly as it showed up, it's gone. The haunting image of the pale face and glowing eyes will forever remain lodged in my head. A horrible scream erupts from the forest, and I scramble to my feet. I run in the direction of the car, or at least where I think the car is. Thousands of thoughts again race through my mind as I move as fast as I can through the woods.

Low-hanging branches and brush cut through my skin. I can't run fast enough. I can't see where I'm going. I'm lost, but I have to keep moving. My chest burns as I gasp for air.

It's behind me; I sense its closeness,

stalking me like prey. Playing a game. Scaring me. I crouch next to a tree to catch my breath. My eyes dart around looking for some sign of escape. And then it happens.

I can hear it breathing heavily, right next to my ear. I close my eyes tight. The fear of knowing I would not be going home fades from my mind, replaced by the terror of what's to come. It touches my skin and turns me around so I can see. I can't comprehend what it is. The long thin legs seem to float just above the ground making this evilness tower over me. Its torso is twisted, and skin hangs loosely from its bones. The eyes peer into me as if searching for my soul.

It bares its teeth, and a low growl seeps from its thin lips. I feel a deep sting as its teeth pierce the soft skin of my shoulder. I can feel the flesh tear away from me. The pain is almost unbearable, and a wave of dizziness passes over me.

I refuse to cry out like Adam. I will not give this thing the satisfaction. I feel cold, and even the darkness around me becomes blurry.

Chapter 1

It's been three years. Three years since my big sis, Cassie, died in the woods.

By the time her body was found by a group of tourists, there wasn't much left of her. She was mostly identified by her iPod and some bits of clothing. Her friends didn't fare much better. The Hunting Woods Massacre: that's what they called it.

The cops never found who did it. They combed Hunting Woods for weeks, months even, and nothing turned up. No fingerprints or pawprints or hoofprints.

There was nothing at all. It's creepy to think that someone — some*thing* — could do all that and not leave a trace. Not a single clue. Eventually, the authorities gave up.

I graduated last year. Cassie should've been there cheering me on. She should've graduated, too. Should've gone off to college. Gotten herself a nice, quiet dormmate. Someone who would've let her listen to her music in peace.

I still have her iPod. Her friend Amanda gave it to her one year for Christmas. The cops gave it to me when they closed the investigation. The screen's cracked. It has a big hole in it, even, and I can't imagine what might've done that. Cassie had a special case on it, and a screen protector. She guarded that thing with her life. It's a hunk of junk now, but it's the last thing I really have of hers, so I keep it. Sometimes I wish it would work, maybe make me feel like she was still here.

Mom and Dad moved away as soon as I graduated. I think they only stayed as long as they did because they didn't want to uproot me. I didn't care, though. Without Cassie, it didn't really matter what school I went to. I think they felt guilty and blamed themselves for her death. They made her go with her friends, even when she said she didn't want to. They said it would be good for her. They should have just let her be. Perhaps I blame them a little myself. I blame her friends more, though.

The music store I work at is going out of business. Downloads and streaming services are taking over. There are some hardcore listeners who come in once in a while, searching for that special vinyl edition of their favorite album, but not enough. Not enough to keep Cassie's favorite place open.

"Hey, Kit! Quit daydreaming and help me box up this shelf!"

My boss snaps me out of my thoughts. Cassie and I were a lot alike that way. We both loved music, loved being alone. I wish we had spent more time alone together. Maybe listening to her collection of albums … Mom and Dad sold them before they moved.

I walk over to Bishop and pick up a box. "Sorry, B. It's getting to be that time of year, you know." My heart still feels heavy with the loss. I don't know how people get over something like this. It's hard to move on.

"Shit, Katherine, I'm sorry." He takes the hair band off his wrist and ties back his dreads to keep them out of his face while he works. "You need a day off? It's not like this crap's going anywhere."

"No." I shake my head. "Cassie would want the music taken care of. I'll be okay. But maybe I can leave early? There's a service tonight at the ranger station."

"Sure."

We work in silence for another couple of hours before the bell over the door rings, signaling a customer.

"Kit! Hey, babe, you ready yet?"

It's Kyle, my boyfriend. Yeah, the alliteration annoys me, too, but you can't help who you fall for. He's into music, too, and he understands me. Can't ask for much more than that. Well, I guess I can ask for that fine ass. And those abs. And those biceps. Mm, perfect drummer's arms.

Cassie would've liked him, I think.

"Go ahead," Bishop says. "I'll close up."

"Thanks, B. Have a good night!" I grab my raggedy messenger bag from behind the counter and reach up on my toes to give Kyle a kiss.

We leave the store and walk out to Kyle's car. It's muggy out, and I try to smooth down my frizzy hair. Curly hair's a bitch in this weather. Kyle's got his arm around me, hand on my hip, his fingers brushing the skin under my T-shirt. I lean into him, grateful to have him with me today. The anniversary of Cassie's death always hits me hard, and since I'm the only family member left, I feel obligated to attend the annual memorial service.

The drive up to the ranger station is short, just twenty minutes, but Kyle still holds my hand the whole time. His band's music is blasting out the car's speakers, and we get more than a few glares from people as we zoom past. Fuck them. They just don't appreciate good music. I rest my arm out the open car window and tap out the rhythm on the door frame.

"You wanna get high before we go in?" Kyle asks.

I look around; the parking lot is pretty much empty. If we roll up the tinted windows of Kyle's van, people will just think we're smoking cigarettes. Or making out. Or fucking. Who cares what people think? Maybe we'll do all three before we go into the ranger station.

We smoke a bowl and fool around for a bit, but just as I'm getting into it, Kyle pulls back and rakes a hand through his jet-black hair. "C'mon. We're gonna be late."

I sigh and pull my T-shirt back on. Damnit. Cock-blocked by mourning.

Hey, maybe that should be the band's new name. Dixie Piss is a crappy band name.

"Good to see you here again this year, Katherine." The head ranger, Mike Compton, tips his hat as I walk in. I hate when people use my full name. I was always Kitty to Cass. Not Kathy. Not Kat. And certainly not Katherine. The only reason I let Bishop get away with it once in a while is because he's cool.

Mike's not cool. Mike is a dick, and if he didn't have a rock-solid alibi for the night Cassie was killed, I'd swear on a stack of vinyl that he did it.

I don't hold much stock in Bibles. Vinyl, though — that shit is the truth.

Kyle shakes Mike's hand, and I notice Mike wince just slightly. Good for Kyle. "Good evening, Mr. Compton. Thanks for hosting the service again. We're not late, are we?" He makes a show of looking at his watch, but Kyle's got the best inner clock of anyone I've ever known. He's still late most of the time, but he knows damn good and well what time it is when he gets where he's going.

"No, Kyle, not at all. We'll always wait for Katherine before we start."

I want to smack that fake sympathetic smile off his ugly face. Fucker.

The service isn't bad, but I notice fewer people each year. Next year, they'll be lucky to have a dozen people. As it is, there are about twenty people milling about, telling stories of the kids as they remembered them. I don't get up to speak. These people didn't like Cassie, weren't nice to her, so I won't be nice to them.

The service comes to an end, and just when I think Kyle and I can safely escape, another ranger walks in and whispers something in Mike's ear. Mike puts two fingers to his mouth and whistles, and everyone gets quiet.

"Ladies and gentlemen, I have grave news. Ranger Thompson here has come to report that there's been another murder in Hunting Woods. As of tonight, the woods are closed off for investigation. Please make your way to the exit in a calm, orderly fashion."

Of course, nobody but me and Kyle is calm or orderly. People start to panic almost instantly, and we have to elbow our way out the door. Everyone wants to stay inside, but I remember the crime scene photos. If whoever — whatever — did that to Cassie is out there, no place is safe. Best for me and Kyle to die in his van together than in this building full of idiots.

Nothing happens on the way to the van, but the air is thicker than ever. I shiver despite the heat, and Kyle puts his arm around me.

Nothing happens on the way to our little studio apartment. We don't say anything for a long time. We just sit there, listening to some techno punk to hide the pounding of our hearts.

I wonder why I'm not more scared. I mean, the thing that killed Cassie might be back. It might be out there, waiting. Not to say that I'm not scared, but I always thought impending doom would be a little more frightening.

No fingerprints. No pawprints. No sign at all, except violent death.

"Who do you think did it, if Mike

didn't?" Kyle's voice startles me, and I almost choke on the inhale.

"I don't know," I answer. "He knows Hunting Woods better than anyone else around here, but nothing about it makes any sense. How could something rip Cass and those other kids apart so bad and not leave a trace?"

Kyle shrugs and takes the joint for a hit of his own. "Maybe it was a demon, man."

"Demons aren't real. That's, like, Christian propaganda. Besides, they leave signs. Sulfur smell, charred remains, stuff like that."

"Says who?"

"TV."

He takes another hit. "Well, maybe this one doesn't. Who the fuck knows?"

My voice comes out a whisper. "Cass. Cass knows."

A ring of pungent smoke punctuates his reply. "That's deep, Kit. Hey, do you think she's out there somewhere? Y'know, another plane or something?"

I think long and hard on it before I

answer. Kyle brings up a good question, one that I don't have an answer for. Is there another life after this one? Everyone always says they hope their loved ones are "out there" looking after them, but where's "out there"? Heaven? Heaven's a crock of shit. I shake my head. "Nope. There's nothing after this miserable hellhole except dirt and decay."

Kyle takes the burned-out roach from my hand and tugs on my arm. "C'mon. Let's go to bed. This shit is depressing to think about."

I don't argue. We leave the music playing, though, because there's no point in life if there's no music. Kyle tries to start something, but I'm not in the mood anymore. I roll over to my other side and let him be the big spoon for the night.

There's an uneasy feeling deep in my gut as I drift off to sleep. I feel like I'm about to remember something important, but before I can I'm out.

Chapter 2

The dream I'm trapped in won't release me. It's amazing how vivid some dreams are, how real they seem. How long they seem to last when you are being tormented by them. I will my eyes to open, but it's not meant to be.

I'm in the woods, and its pitch black. However, I can see everything. I have perfect night vision. I'm perched in the top of a tree looking across the forest. I'm watching a small rodent forage through the brush on the ground looking for food. Hunting. It stops moving, and its ears twitch, eyes locked on a bush in front of it. After a moment, it grabs something and scurries off. We are both predictors tonight.

I hear something in the distance. It catches my attention, and I look away from the hunt below me. This is something for me, and I'm going to make it mine. I take a deep breath and lift my head. I exhale and sniff the air once more. I smell the faint scent of blood. As it grows stronger, my stomach begins to ache. I can feel it churning. Longing for just a taste. That's all I want. The need grows, and I become angry. The smell of blood always sets me off. I lose control of my emotions.

I catch a glimpse of the creature, limping down a small dirt trail that's almost overgrown. He must have hurt his leg out here and is trying to make it home. These woods can be difficult to navigate, especially at night. There's no way he'll make it out of here now. It doesn't seem like he has much fight in him either. It looks like he has pretty much given up.

My body moves, and I glide down the tree to begin the chase. It's like I'm floating. My body moves with ease. My limbs move differently than I'm used to. I'm faster. More agile. It's freeing. Like I'm not even touching the ground.

I move quickly, weaving around the trees. My senses tell me that my prey's right in front of me. A twig snaps under me, and we both stop. He can't see me, but I see him, standing still, listening to the sounds of the night. I step out from the brush that's hiding me and stand in front of him. His face contorts, and I see the fear. His short black hair moves in the breeze. His heart begins to race. I hear it thumping in his chest. It sounds like it's about to burst.

I begin circling him. The creature takes off, trying to run away. Feet hitting the ground so hard I can hear the pounding. I play with him, letting him have just a little bit of distance between us. The chase doesn't last long, however. After just a few moments he slows his pace; his energy's depleted, and his leg's beginning to drag the ground.

I hear his breathing coming in gasps now. He's made this easy.

I see his figure as he crouches down, leaning himself against a tree. Body shivering. My long limbs stretch out as I try to slow my pace, sliding almost into him. Without stopping to think, I sink my teeth into him, and my fingers, now like claws, tear into his skin. It only takes a moment. His body is shredded. A growl of pleasure escapes my mouth.

"Kit, wake up!" I hear Kyle's voice breaking through the darkness. "Babe, look at me. You're dreaming."

I open my eyes. Kyle's hands are on my shoulders and he's partially shaking me, partially holding me down. My head's pounding. My body is slick with sweat. The sheets cling to me, and the breeze from the fan chills my flesh. The dream's still fresh in my head. It was exhilarating yet horrifying. My heart feels like it's about to jump out of my ribcage.

I glance at Kyle and notice bright red scratches across his chest.

"Oh my God! What happened?"

"You attacked me in your sleep. I've been trying to wake you up for the last ten minutes, Kit."

"It was horrible! T-the woods …" I stammer over my words. "I was some k-kind of…" I shake my head trying to get rid of the images. I feel like I can't breathe. My adrenaline is peaked, and my emotions are getting the best of me.

"That must've been one hell of a dream," Kyle interrupts me. "You just came at me. Your eyes were open, but you were still asleep. It was freaky, babe!"

"I'm so sorry. I didn't mean to."

A million thoughts hit me all at once. Was this what happened to my sister and her friends? Did it happen that fast? Did she suffer? I can't stand the thought of her suffering.

This wasn't the first time I've had a dream like this, but it's been a long time, and never as the hunter. I've had a ton of dreams where something was chasing me. This changed everything. Made it more intense. More real. I couldn't even put into words what I saw and experienced in this dream.

I feel sick to my stomach, and I jump out of bed and rush to the bathroom.

Moments later I walk back into the bedroom, wiping tears from my eyes. Nothing could make this day worse.

There's no way I'd be able to get those visions out of my head. I'm miserable, and Kyle can tell.

I glance at the clock and realize it's a little past eight a.m. I should be getting ready for work. Instead, I sit back down on the bed and lean into Kyle. The tears come again slowly, and I break. He pulls me into him and wraps himself around me, arms squeezing me tight. He kisses my forehead.

"I'm going to call Bishop. Tell him you're not going to be in today." I don't respond. I don't want to talk. I just want to crawl back into bed, turn on a funny movie, and try to escape my mind at this point. I unwrap myself from him and pick up the remote. As soon as the TV comes on, the news is blasting a story about the recent discovery in Hunting Woods.

"A body was discovered in Hunting Woods yesterday," the news anchor announces in a monotone voice. He has a blank stare and shows no emotion. "The unidentified man was found by Hunting

Lake in the evening by a group of young kids. There are no details yet on how long he was out there, however, it appears this murder may be linked to the massacre that took place three years ago at this time. Until further notice, the woods are to be considered very dangerous and no one should venture out there." His voice drones on. "Local officials ask for everyone to stay away from the area until further notice. If anyone has any information regarding this incident, please call your local police …"

And just like that, they move on to another story about a new local dog bakery that's going into the shopping center around the corner. I change the channel. I can't bear to think about that right now. The murder, that is.

They will never know what happened out there. Just like with my sister and her friends. They will give up the search for clues, and people will slowly forget.

Kyle lights up a joint and passes it to me.

"Looks like you could use this right

now, Kit."

I think about turning him down but decide I need something to cut through this somber mood I have been forced into. Maybe it will let me sleep without the crazy dream. I'm exhausted; it feels like I haven't slept in days.

After a few hits I lay back on the bed, placing my head against Kyle's chest. I listen to his heart for a few moments before closing my eyes.

I don't dream anymore, but my sleep the rest of the morning is restless and choppy. I finally wake up about ten thirty with a massive headache. A couple of pills I saved from having my wisdom teeth pulled do the trick, but I can't get the dream from earlier off my mind.

There's a note on the nightstand. Kyle left for band practice while I was asleep.

See ya tonight, babe. B says you're good to stay home today. He'll watch the store for you. If you get it in your stubborn head to go anywhere alone today, take that knife I got you for Christmas or something. Stay safe. Love you, K.

I chuckle when I read about the knife. Kyle got the thing in a pawn shop last year and saved it for the holiday to give me. It was for self defense, he said. He said he couldn't picture me spraying an attacker with mace like a little bitch, but he could definitely see me stabbing the fucker.

It's the coolest knife I've ever seen. It's got a bone handle with silver inlay, and the designs carved into the wicked curved blade look like some ancient writing. Super cool, but not very practical. I mean, the thing is big and heavy, and it didn't come with a sheath. Kyle made one out of some old leather he found at the same pawn shop. The sheath fits the knife like a glove. Kyle's really good with his hands ... *really* good. But still, I don't think I'm going to be lugging that knife around if I leave the apartment. It's sweet of him to think of me like that, though.

I spend a couple hours puttering around the apartment, tidying up. I flush the roaches, stash the stash, and wash all the dirty dishes. It doesn't take long enough; I'm itchy and twitchy, wanting something to do to take my mind off the dream.

After twenty minutes of tapping my feet and nibbling on my nails, I decide I won't calm down any time soon. Best to do something productive. I grab my bag and head for the place that always soothes me — the cemetery.

Chapter 3

Now, I'm not one of those goth chicks who's all morbid and spends half their time in graveyards and stuff. I just miss Cass something fierce, and talking to her helps sometimes.

The cemetery's on the other side of town, away from the woods. I have no problem being away from the woods right now. Let murderous someone — or something — have a go at the idiot kids who will, without a doubt, head straight for the danger just to get a rush. I'll stay safe, thank you very much.

Despite the fact that the knife is cumbersome, I take it after all. Just to be sure.

Cass has a pretty nice headstone. I have to give Mom and Dad credit for that. They really shelled out. Elaborate angel statue, engraved music notes ... I think they were trying to compensate for the fact that they knew they were going to leave her here all alone. Not me. I stayed.

Mom said the headstone and burial cleaned out Cassie's college fund. I guess it must have sucked to have saved so much for your kid's future only for that future to be snuffed out. No, that's not right. Snuffed out makes it sound peaceful, like a candle going out. Cass didn't go peaceful. Her future wasn't snuffed out — it was ripped to shreds.

"Hey, Cass," I say as I sit down on top of her grave. I set her old iPod down next to my smartphone and tap the phone's screen until her old Pandora list pops up. Indie rock. I don't know what I'll do if Pandora goes out of business. They've got

Cassie's soul in their database; my only connection, since the iPod's toast.

A couple people in the cemetery give me sideways glances when I start talking. Fuck them. People talk to the dead all the time. Not my fault their dead don't talk back.

Let me backtrack a second. Cass doesn't, like, literally talk back to me. No, she uses the Pandora station to communicate with me. Sometimes that station will play the most random shit, stuff that Cassie wouldn't normally listen to, but stuff that makes perfect sense in the context of our conversation.

I wonder sometimes if I'm a hypocrite for saying that there's nothing after death when I come to talk to Cass at least two, three times a week. The shrink my parents sent me to after her death said it's a normal coping mechanism. Whatever.

"So another person was killed in Hunting Woods last night," I say. She doesn't have TV anymore, so she wouldn't know yet. Better to get the bad news out of the way right off. "Just like you. They're not saying serial killer yet, but I bet it's on everyone's mind. This whole town's gonna be talking about that kind of thing soon enough, so I figure I'd be the one to break it to you before the rumor mill gets out of hand.

"I wish you could tell me what happened. I mean, I know you can't, but it would be nice to have some closure, y'know? To know if it was a person or a thing that did that to you."

The song ends, and a new song plays. *Out of This World* by Beatnik Bards. A chill runs down my spine.

"That's pretty creepy, Cass. Are you sure? I mean, it's not like you to exaggerate, so I guess you are. Anyway, I guess it makes sense, what with the dream I had. Oh! I should tell you about my dream. It was wild." I launch into a narrative about the nightmare from the night before. *Out of This World* ends, and *I Told You So* by The Hot Toddies starts up. "Yeah, yeah, I know. But it can't be real, can it? I mean, the monster from my dream ... That's TV bullshit. Not real life."

Now Pandora plays *Little Bit Crazy* by K. Flay. That one stings.

"C'mon, Cass, I'm trying to keep an open mind here, but some things just aren't possible. I'm not crazy. I'm being realistic."

The song changes mid-beat, and I'm starting to get annoyed with Cassie. "Really, Cassie? *Asylum*? That's bullshit." I pick up the iPod and phone and stuff them in my bag. "I'll come back when you're not in such a bitchy mood."

I hate when Cass and I fight. It's worse now that she's dead because she always gets the last word.

Cass is buried pretty far into the cemetery, so I always pass by the other kids' graves on the way back to my car. I get anxious when I walk past them, because I think they know I blame them for Cassie's death. They shouldn't have made her come on that stupid camping trip.

I wasn't talking to Cass for very long, but it's late in the day by the time I leave.

Not dark yet, because it's summer, but the mugginess in the air has changed. The wind picks up, and my frizz-tastic hair gets even more out-of-control. I tie it back with an elastic band and tug the hood of my jacket over my head. A storm's coming, and it feels like a bad one.

Rain starts pounding on the windshield about halfway home. I turn on the wipers and squint into the foggy mess that has risen from the rain hitting the hot pavement. A couple of near-misses later, and I'm home. Fucking jackasses on the road today.

Kyle's van is in its parking space when I get back. Band practice must've ended early. I hope he's not worried that I was gone when he came home.

I stomp the water off my soggy shoes when I get inside and lock the door behind me. I'm surprised to see the apartment is lit with candles, and Kyle's got dinner ready. Steak and potatoes, and he managed to scrounge up some decent wine.

"What's the occasion?" I say as I set

down my bag.

Kyle wraps his arms around me and rests his chin on top of my head. "You've had a shit day, so I thought I'd end it on an up note."

"You didn't have to do all this."

He kisses me deep, and I can't help but sigh. "I know I didn't *have* to," he says. "I wanted to."

We eat in silence, and Kyle passes me a joint when we're done. "Go to visit Cass again today?"

"Yeah," I say. Kyle doesn't mind that I talk to Cassie. Sometimes he'll come with and just listen to me talk to her. Sometimes he talks to her, too. I think it helps that Kyle's a musician; he understands her language. "She was in a mood today. Called me crazy after I told her about my dream."

"Well, what does she know? She's not the one who had the dream."

"Exactly!"

"You going to go to work tomorrow?"

I think about it before I answer. "I guess. I mean, even if I have another crazy dream, I've gotta get paid. I don't have any cool gigs lined up like you do." I nudge his shoulder with mine.

"I keep telling you, we could use some new vocals on some of our tracks. I think you'd be great."

"You're just saying that because I'm your girlfriend."

He shakes his head. "I would never lie about music. You've got a great voice, Kit. You just need to get out there on stage and let the rest of the world hear it."

I sit and stare into a candle flame for a while before I answer. Kyle knows I don't like getting up in front of people to sing. I had a massive panic attack at karaoke night last year, and that was after a few drinks to loosen me up. "I'd have to be wasted beyond belief to get up on stage, Kyle. I get too nervous."

"Okay. I won't push you."

Kyle pulls me in close, and for a couple of hours I'm able to forget the world and my problems.

Hours later, my phone rings, and I can barely breathe to answer it. Just like I figured, the neighbors complained. I tell the landlord we'll turn the TV down, and Kyle lights up a cigarette. We take turns smoking ourselves back to reality.

I don't dream that night—or if I do, I don't remember it. Kyle doesn't wake me up from any nightmares, and he doesn't have fresh scratches on him in the morning. Maybe whatever got into my head at the news of the latest murder in Hunting Woods finally is gone.

Maybe I'm fooling myself.

Chapter 4

"Hey Christine, you want to go out with a few of us tonight?" A scrawny-but-cute curly-haired boy says. He nudges his friend with his elbow to make sure he has her attention. His hair falls just over his ears, and he tries to flip it out of his face. It doesn't take long before it's hanging in his eyes again.

"I don't know. Where you guys off to?" is the response from his little female friend. She runs her finger over one of the few albums left on the shelf. Neither of them appears to be a collector. Probably just passing time until their show starts at the theater across the street.

"A group of us are heading out to the woods after it gets dark." He lowers his voice a bit. "We want to see if we find anything." He tries to do a spooky laugh and fails.

Unable to hold back, I hear myself interrupt their conversation. "Are you guys fucking crazy? Are you wanting to end up dead?" At first, the two of them remain silent. Maybe they are pondering the words I've said and realize it's a bad idea.

Then ...

"I think you need to stop being nosy!" the girl snaps in a snooty, know-it-all tone. "Why don't you just do your job and see if you have that record I asked for?"

"We're just gonna have some fun. It's no big deal," he adds to her statement.

I just shake my head. So far it has been an uneventful day at work. Moving some boxes out. The last few customers making their rounds, trying to find killer deals on the remaining vinyl left in the store. Most of the good stuff's packed up though; Bishop's going to keep it.

"Well, what you see on the shelves is what we have left. So you'll have to get it somewhere else. And my sister and her friends tried to have fun out there, and all of them wound up dead. I hope you have better luck, assholes."

"You're lucky this shitty store is closing because if it wasn't, I'd have you fired."

I take a step toward her, and before I know it Bishop is in the middle of us, stopping a fight before it starts. "I will kindly ask you to leave the store. We are closing up in a minute." He stands directly in front of me, his back facing me so he can exchange words with the customers. "I thank you for stopping by."

The girl gives me another dirty look, flipping me off as they make their way out of the store. I'm sure I'll catch her somewhere later and we can finish our conversation then.

"I'm glad you waited until the last day of the store being open to tell a customer off," Bishop says as he turns around and looks at me, a smile playing around his lips. I'm sure it wasn't the first time, but I'm glad he thinks so.

"They're stupid. They were talking about going out to the woods tonight." I look at him, and he's got his hand over his mouth, trying not to laugh. "It's not funny. What if something happens to them?"

"You're right. Maybe you should call it in. Just in case."

I think about it for a moment, then decide to let it go. If they want to risk their lives, then so be it. Calling it in won't stop them. I let out a deep sigh and lean against the counter.

"I don't know what I'm going to do after today, B. With this place closed, I feel like a part of the town is dying. There will never be a job as cool as this."

"The town will go on. Just like before. Stores close all the time."

"I'm going to miss it, though."

"Me too," he says as he hands me an album. "I want you to have this one, it was Cassie's favorite." The cardboard sleeve is black and grey and says Taco Mouth across the top. "She played that album non-stop."

"Yeah. They were on her playlist. I always wondered what a Taco Mouth was."

He laughs out loud as he walks to the door and locks it. "Well, that's all she wrote my friend." A somber tone hits his voice. "I'll let you out the back door. I can finish the small stuff that's left tomorrow."

I grab my coat and the vinyl he gave me and follow him to the back of the building. I make the trip home as quickly as possible. Lucky for me there's very little traffic on the roads.

I sit silent most of the evening, listening to the Taco Mouth record Bishop gave me and thinking of Cassie. Thinking about the kids in the store today who are about to make a huge mistake. It weighs heavy on me.

"Why so quiet tonight, babe?" Kyle breaks the silence. He sits down next to me on the couch and leans into me. The warmth of his body usually calms me, but tonight it doesn't do anything to soothe my anxiety.

"Just thinking about some stupid kids in the store today. They were talking about going into the woods tonight." I look towards the window and see that it's gotten dark out. "They're probably out there right now."

"I don't know ... maybe they got scared and didn't go. You're probably worrying for nothing."

"What if they're out there right now, though? They won't make it out. Not if ..." I stop mid-sentence, unable to even get the words out of my mouth. I can't even imagine what it is out there killing people. "I'm about to suggest the stupidest thing ever, but maybe we should drive by and make sure no one is there. I would feel better knowing they didn't go."

"You're right, that's pretty stupid. I'm

with you though. If it makes you feel better, I'll drive you."

Once again, I'm left feeling lucky to have him in my life. Who else would offer to go to a place like that?

I go over everything in my head. I know we shouldn't go, but worrying about the little jerks from the store won't let me rest. I stand up and grab my jacket, deciding I won't get any sleep if I keep thinking about it. Kyle follows behind. He grabs a small flashlight from the counter as we exit the apartment.

"Just in case. You never know when you'll need one of these." He puts it in his pocket and locks the door behind him.

Twenty minutes later, we pull into the parking lot.

"Well, I guess they didn't chicken out," Kyle remarks as we park close to the ranger station. There's a blue van parked near the start of the trail. Kyle rolls down his window, and we glance out into the distance. It's black and menacing. If anything's out there, it will be almost impossible to see it from here.

A flash of light catches my attention. My gaze into the darkness intensifies, trying to catch a glimpse of the light again. After a minute I see it again.

"Over there. I saw a light." I point to Kyle's left-hand side, and he begins to search for the light as well. The speck of light shines a little brighter now, moving in erratic motions. He puts his hand on the door and opens it. Before he can get out of the car, a scream erupts from inside the woods. Without even thinking, he's out of the car and running toward the sound. As he runs, he pulls the flashlight from his pocket and turns it on.

"Kyle, stop! Don't be stupid!" I yell after him, but it's too late. He's already at the trail and heading into the woods. "Shit!" I mumble to myself as I stand by the car, debating what I should do. The thought of heading into the woods frightens me; however, not only are those kids in there, Kyle's now in there as well.

As I near the edge of the woods, I get out my phone and place a call to the police department.

"Nine-one-one emergency. How can I help you?"

"There's some kids out in Hunting Woods. I heard screaming, like something was attacking them. My boyfriend ran out there to try and help them."

"What part of the woods ma'am?"

"We're near the ranger station. I don't know how far in the woods they are. I noticed a light, and I can hear screams here and there, but—"

"Just stay where you are, okay? Don't go into the woods. Someone will be out there shortly. Just stay on the phone with me."

"But my boyfriend's in there. He went to help those kids. I can't let him stay in there alone."

"I understand that, ma'am, but having an extra person lost in the woods isn't good, either. Stay where you are. Help is on the way."

Before I can say anything else my phone goes dead. "Damn it." It was fully charged. What happened to it? Another scream from inside the woods makes me jump. It sounds like a female. How many of them went out there?

"Cassie, I really wish you were here right now. I could use you."

I debate for a moment about what I should do, then I start down the path. I can't leave Kyle out there. He's here because of me. He would never leave me out there alone, no matter what was there. My whole body's shaking despite my resolve.

Out of nowhere, two kids come barreling down the dirt path at me, full speed, one almost knocking me over. Instead, he falls to the ground. His friend continues running, not even looking back.

"It got them," he cries, tears streaming down his face. He's caked with dirt.

"What got them?"

He doesn't respond. He jumps up and continues running to get out of the woods. His friend is already long gone.

I look away from the direction the kids left in and back down the path. "Kyle, where are you?" I yell out into the blackness. I creep down the narrow dirt track. I can't see anything, and with my phone going dead, I can't even use that as a flashlight. I hear a rustling sound and twigs snapping right in front of me. I stop, trying to get my eyes to adjust, trying to see something. Anything at all would be nice.

"Kyle, is ... is that you?" My voice seems so small now.

Nothing. No response.

Again, I hear the same sound, only closer to me. A figure begins to form, but I can't make it out. The darkness eats up my view of anything. Deep breathing penetrates the night.

"Kyle?"

A disfigured mass comes at me, its eyes glowing bright. It knocks me back against a tree, and my head hits the trunk. I don't know if my vision is blurry or if it's the dark playing tricks on my eyes.

I can feel it breathing down my neck. Is this what happened to Cassie? Am I going to end up like her and her friends?

I should have just let those kids come out here and not even worried about any of them. I know, however, that the guilt would have killed me if anything happened to them, and I did nothing.

I feel a pain in my chest, hot and searing, and then a bright light fills the air right above me. In the light I can see Cassie's face. It hovers above for a moment, lighting up the night. I see the thing that is attacking me. A grotesque creature, part human ... part monster.

"What the fuck are you?" I ask. I feel like it has its hand wrapped around my heart, squeezing. I try to catch my breath.

The light circling above my head shoots down at me. A warmth fills my body. I feel peace. It's like Cassie wrapped her arms around me and embraced me. Then the darkness returns, and I slip into unconsciousness.

When my eyes open again, the light of the morning is shining through the trees, and I hear people calling out. A tan dog comes trotting across the woods at me, barking loudly, his tail wagging. Right behind him are a bunch of local cops.

"Ma'am, don't move. It looks like you're hurt. You're lucky to be alive; a few others weren't so lucky."

I can't think. My head spins, and I feel the darkness taking over again.

* * *

I open my eyes to find myself in a hospital bed. Kyle stands beside me, holding my hand. He brushes some stray hairs out of my face and kisses my forehead.

"You gave us all a scare, babe. You fell and hit your head pretty hard when you were walking into work."

"What? No, we went to the woods. There were kids out there. We tried to help them. Cassie was there." I realize how ridiculous it sounds when I say it out loud. It seemed so real though.

"Cassie's been gone for a long time, Kit. You must have been dreaming. You were unconscious for almost two days. It was just a dream. Everything is fine."

"It was so real. The creature. Cassie. I couldn't find you. You ran off trying to help some kids. It was so dark, and you were gone."

"Well, I'm here now, and there's no creature. Just relax. Watch some TV." He picks up the remote and turns the channel on the television mounted to the wall across from my bed.

"Breaking news: Two teenagers have been found dead this morning near the south end of Hunting Woods. The victims have not yet been identified, but eyewitness reports state that what was left of the bodies can possibly be identified as a male and a female victim. We will keep you updated as we receive more information. For the time being, authorities are asking citizens to please heed their advice and avoid the woods until these gruesome crimes are solved.

"Carlton Heights chief of police, Roger Bullman, issued this statement earlier today—"

"Please turn it off, Kyle. I can't … with my dream I just can't hear that right now."

He fumbles with the remote to change

the channel again, but it's the same broadcast on every station. The dream doesn't want to end. He turns the TV off and takes my hand.

"Just close your eyes and try to rest some more, babe. It will get better if you get some more sleep."

I disagree. My sleep has been tormenting me these past couple of days. At this point I'm scared to close my eyes. The nurse comes in and checks on me, giving me some medication to help with the pain in my head. The meds help with the headache, but I still don't want to sleep. I fight the effects of the pills as long as I can, but when Kyle climbs into the hospital bed next to me and wraps me in his arms, I'm out like a light.

I don't dream again that night, a fact that calms me a bit when the morning comes. Kyle moved to the chair next to the bed sometime during the night, probably to give me room to be more comfortable. His snoring is soft, and I almost don't want to wake him, except his neck is crooked at a terrible angle. I know it's going to be hard for him to play tonight's set if he's got a stiff neck from sleeping too long in that chair.

"Kyle. Kyle!"

He jerks awake, looks around, and for a second I wonder if he had the same sort of dream I did — that all-too-real, disorienting, what-day-is-it kind of dream.

"Morning, babe," he says as he stretches. He's wearing a tight white T-shirt, and I can see the muscles flex under the fabric. "How'd you sleep?"

I rub my neck, embarrassed to have gotten so confused after my mini-coma. "Much better, thanks. No crazy dreams."

"Good," he says. He stands up and leans over to give me a kiss on the forehead. "The nurse wanted to know when you woke up, so they could do some testing. You feeling up to it, or do you want to eat something first?"

Despite my reprieve from dreaming and despite going so long without food, I don't really feel hungry. I ask for some breakfast anyway, because I know my headache will only get worse if I don't eat something.

I almost regret it when the tray comes to my room. Grits, gravy, and a biscuit. Carb city.

A little while later, once the tray has been taken away, a nurse comes to take me for the testing. I sit through X-rays and CAT scans and an MRI that seems to take forever. When I'm wheeled back to my room, I see that I have more visitors.

"Mom. Dad. What are you guys doing here?"

Chapter 5

I'm a little surprised to see my folks. I've gotten birthday and Christmas cards since they left, but they haven't stopped by. They don't call. Except for the times when I'm thinking about when Cassie was alive, I've almost forgotten that I even have parents.

Kyle excuses himself to give us some privacy, promising to bring back something edible from the cafeteria. I'm left alone with the two people who abandoned me the second I graduated, who couldn't wait to leave the town

Cassie grew up in — the town Cassie died in.

"Kitty, how can you ask us why we're here? Kyle called us when you were brought to the hospital. Of course, we'd come to see how you're doing. We were worried sick."

I bite my tongue to keep from biting my mom's head off. Kyle said I was out for two days. If I take the time to do the math, that means today's Saturday.

They couldn't even be bothered to take a couple days off work to come see me. In the fucking hospital.

I cross my arms over my chest. "Well, as you can see, I'm fine now. Just had some tests done, and when the results come in I'll probably be free of this joint. So you can go back to your lives now. No need to pretend you give a shit."

"Katherine! Don't you dare talk to your mother like that. We've both been worried about you, so much so that Mary's hardly slept since Kyle called."

"But not so much that you'd take time off your stupid jobs to come down."

Dad takes a step closer. "We just got back here from your apartment — where Kyle graciously allowed us to stay once we got into town, which, by the way, was a couple hours after we found out about your accident. We have been going back there at night because the hospital only allows one overnight visitor, and that boy won't leave your side for the world."

I feel my skin go hot, and I know I'm blushing. I should be. I'm an asshole.

I look down at my hands in my lap. Normally, I don't have a problem finding the words I want to say. Now, though, I'm so mortified I can't even come up with a good snarky comeback.

It's quiet in the room for a while — too quiet. Mom's the first to speak up again.

"We saw the news, Kitty. We know this has got to be a tough time for you. We just want to make sure you're okay." She walks over and puts a hand on my shoulder. I fight the urge to shrug it off. I have to keep telling myself that she's trying, and that's more than she's done in a year.

"Yeah, I'm great. People are getting murdered again, just like Cass, and the record store's gonna close soon." I feel tears slip from my eyes, and it makes me angrier than seeing Mom and Dad did. I shouldn't be crying. I'm tougher than that. Cassie would want me to be tougher than that. Still, the tears come, and before I know it, I'm bawling and hiccupping, and Mom's kneeling down next to the wheelchair, holding me like I was a little kid again. "Mom, they were already starting to forget her, and now this new shit is going to wipe her out of existence. Everyone's going to be focused on these new kids getting killed, and no one's gonna remember that Cassie went through it, too, that she was one of the first."

"Honey, no one's going to forget Cassie."

"Mom, Cass says whatever killed her isn't natural."

More silence from my parents. Mom tenses up, and even though I'm looking down, I bet they're giving each other that "look" over my head. I know the look without even seeing it. It's the same look they gave me when I first told them about Cass's Pandora station. It was also the last time I told them about her Pandora station.

I pull away from Mom. "Never mind."

Mom sits back on her heels. Her brows are all scrunched up, like she's confused about something. "Kit, is there something you want to tell us?"

There are a lot of things I want to tell them. "Go to hell" is at the top of the list. But I just shake my head, grateful that Kyle has returned with sausage and bacon and some much-needed coffee.

With Kyle in the room, Dad's less of an ass, and Mom doesn't hover. They make small talk while I feign a headache, so I don't have to talk. After a couple of awkward hours, my test results come back: I'm about as normal as I'm ever going to get. No tumor, no hemorrhage, no stroke, just a concussion. Mom makes some excuse about having to get back to

Boston. Dad grumbles something that sounds like "Love you, Kitty" as they walk out the door, but I know that can't be right.

Since I'm doing well, the doc says I can leave. It takes another couple of hours for the paperwork to go through, but since it's just Kyle and me the tension eases up, and I can breathe again.

Kyle drives me to my car, a beat-up yellow Beetle that used to belong to Cassie, then follows me home. Most people might feel creeped out with a van following behind them in their rear-view mirror, but since it's Kyle's face in the driver seat I feel safer.

We get home, and Kyle locks the bolt and chain. I plop facedown on the bed, exhausted. I feel Kyle's weight settle on the bed beside me, and his hands massage my shoulders. He knows exactly where all my knots are, and he works them out like magic. I feel relaxed, really relaxed, for the first time since I woke up in the hospital.

I wait for Kyle's hands to move below

my waist, but instead he lies down next to me and pulls me close. I'm the little spoon again, and it feels so right.

"I can't believe Mom and Dad just left like that. They could've stayed a day or two, gone to visit Cassie." A single tear slides down my cheek, and I sniffle in spite of myself. "She misses them; she told me so. Did you know they haven't gone to see her since the funeral? Not even to see the gravestone once it was up."

Kyle kisses the top of my head and hugs me closer. "I know, babe, but you gotta remember that they lost Cassie, too. Maybe they just don't know how to talk to her like you do. Maybe they feel guilty for letting her go on the trip, or maybe they think she blames them."

We lie like that for the rest of the night, but I don't sleep. I can't. I need to see Cass, to tell her I saw Mom and Dad, but by the time I got discharged, the cemetery was closed.

Tomorrow. Tomorrow I'll talk to Cassie and let her know what's going on.

Maybe she'll have some answers for me.

* * *

Sundays the cemetery is usually packed, but today there's a storm rolling in and most people have stayed home. I tried to keep my hair in line with a tight braid, but already I've got wayward curls blowing in my face.

"So that's pretty much it. Mom tried to make up for lost time, and Dad was a dick—as usual. It's like he was mad at me for getting hurt. Fuck, it's not like I did it on purpose. I don't even know how I fell. Kyle said Bishop found me in the alley out behind the store. I've got a huge knot on my forehead. It's sore, but don't worry, Cass, I'm okay. Your little sis is too tough to let a little concussion keep her down."

Talk to Me by the Thunder Ballroom is playing.

"Yeah, I had a dream again while I was unconscious. It was even more real than the other one. In this dream, the monster got me. It got me this time, Cass. It had its claws around my heart, but you saved me. You were there, Cass." I sigh and brush more hair out of my face. A light rain starts to fall, so I pull up my hoodie and zip it all the way to my neck. It's still hot as balls out, especially with the humidity, but I've got goosebumps.

The song finishes, and a new one comes on. I'm not familiar with this song, so I check my phone. The title is *Heaven on Earth*, and the band name is one I don't recognize. I Google it and find out that the song was just released last week.

It's not the first time Cassie has been more in-touch with the current music scene than I am, but I shudder just the same. "Cass, there's no such thing as heaven. It's just some made-up place the religious nutjobs talk about to keep people in line. Heaven, hell — it's all fake, Cassie. All of that shit."

I tune back in to the last few lyrics as the song finishes, and my heart starts racing.

> *It's something that I never knew*
> *Before you left this world*
> *Heaven's not a place above*

> *For good little boys and girls*
> *Heaven's here, heaven's now*
> *It's real, and it's a truth*
> *But heaven on Earth will never come*
> *Until I'm back with you*

Tears fill my eyes, and I wipe them with the back of my hand. "That's what I'm scared of, Cass. I'm scared that these dreams will come true, and I'll be in heaven on Earth with you—dead."

My other hand is on my bag, and I can feel the lump of the knife inside. Hunting Woods are on the other side of town, but I don't feel right without that knife on me at all times. The air has an electricity to it, and the clouds hanging low above are ominous. I have a bad feeling about tonight.

Just as I'm saying my good-byes and reaching down to shut off the music app, one final song starts to play.

> *It's cold, it's dark*
> *I feel it now*
> *The knife inside my heart*
> *With every beat*
> *With every breath*
> *It slices me apart*

It's not until
The knife comes out
I realize that I've killed
That part of me
That poisoned beat
The demon's heart is stilled

Chapter 6

Another day, another murder (or two) in the woods.

This time it's a male and a female, both seventeen years old. The remains of one body is found a few miles in, close to the lake. They haven't identified him yet. Not much left, just like the others. They are lucky to even find him.

The female, it appears, almost made it out of that hell. Her body, which is almost all intact, is found at the edge of the woods. So close, just a few more feet and she would have been all right.

Her name was Skylar. Speculation is the male victim may have been her boyfriend. However, they have to do more research to know for sure. Check dental records, that kind of thing. I wonder if these kids were the ones in my dream the other night. Just from reading the description in the paper, it's like reliving the details of my nightmare.

My dreams keep getting worse. The creature, or whatever it is, is getting clearer to me. The glowing eyes, the long limbs, the pasty white flesh. Just the thought of it sends shivers down my spine. I haven't been able to put it into words to tell Kyle. How do you describe something so horrific?

The images of every dream haunt me for days, and the more I dream, the more death follows behind. I can't stop them from coming, though. Even when I'm awake, it seems as if I'm stuck in a dream. Flashbacks every time I see the news on TV or read the paper.

It seems as if the teens in town have

created a new game to see who's brave enough to venture out into the woods. After the first death, you'd think they would learn. I wonder if the prize at the end is worth it, if any of them can make it out, that is.

The police have issued warnings and even begun arresting anyone they see heading into the woods. But still, they are slipping through. You can't really cover that much area with the small police force this town has. There are so many spots to park and enter the woods. Nothing can be done to stop it.

I let out a sigh, too tired to show more of a reaction, while reading through the article. Kyle already knows. He can read me. The tension in my body. Kyle, even though he's been supportive, has begun sleeping on the couch some nights because, with the night terrors, come more scratches and bruises for him.

"You alright, babe?"

"Yeah. These kids are so stupid." Another sigh escapes me. "Cassie tries to tell me about what's happening to them, and I can't stop it. I don't know what to do. If I go to the cops, they'll all think I'm crazy. No one will believe my dead sister talks to me."

Out of nowhere the record player begins blasting. Kyle jumps a little as he turns to look at the device that had been off only moments ago. Cassie's been more active, coming through any chance she gets. I like her being around because I miss her terribly; however, I don't like what it means when she shows up.

Kyle has to believe me when stuff like that happens. There's no way to deny something supernatural is at work. She must be comfortable with him being around now. Before she would only talk to me when I'd visit her.

He shakes himself off and looks at me. "Well, you know, I have the day off. Maybe I can help you relax for a few.": He smiles at me and runs his fingers through my tangled hair, leaning in. I feel his lips press against mine.

A sultry song begins to stream through the speakers, and we look into each other's eyes. After a moment laughter breaks the silence, and Kyle stands up, taking my hand as he leads me over to the bed.

We fit together so perfectly, and it's not long before I'm screaming so loud that the landlord comes pounding on the door.

Once Kyle has smooth-talked the landlord — with pants on, of course — we snuggle on the bed, bathing in the afterglow. I take a long hit from Kyle's pipe and begin to cough. Tears well up in my eyes, and I feel my lungs burning. He laughs at me and pokes my side.

"Take it easy."

"Sorry, just trying to get out of my head." I take another hit. "Stay in here tonight, please. I don't want to be alone."

He takes the pipe back from me and shakes his head. "You're not going to beat me up tonight, are ya? I still have bruises from the last time I slept in here."

"Shut up. You know I feel bad about that." I give him a sideways glance. "And I can't promise anything."

He places his pipe on the table next to the bed and lies back, pulling me with him. I lay my head on his chest and close my eyes, my hand resting on his stomach. It would be nice being close to him tonight. I'm quick to fall asleep, and the dreams start just as fast.

I'm staring down at a broken body, limbs twisted at angles that shouldn't be possible. Dull eyes look up at me. Blood trickles down from the mouth. I almost feel sorry for the poor soul, but they put themselves here. They made the choice to come out into the woods.

The woods ...

I'm back in the woods. I feel myself begin to panic. I look up from the body on the ground and peer out into the darkness. If I could just wake myself up, everything would be all right.

A light dances in the distance, and I'm being pulled towards it. Deeper and deeper into tree-filled land. The ball of light floats closer to me, hovering in the night air right in front of my face, slowly making a circle around my head and then it flashes. Out of the light comes a figure. Cassie, transparent but in full form.

I hear her say my name, and then she motions for me to follow her. Slowly, moving off the path. I want to turn away and go back, but I can't stop myself. After several moments I hear voices. Two men talking low. One raspy voice whispering to the other.

"Richard, we have to catch this thing. We can't let any more of our kids die out here."

"I know, believe me, I know. It won't do anyone any good, though, if we die out here."

"We're getting that son of a bitch tonight. I'm doing it with or without you. I'm not letting these woods take any more of our kids. It ends tonight."

Richard looks out, trying to see past the trees, and bobs his head up and down. "I know, Jason. I have your back. I just — I have a bad feeling, y'know?"

Cassie is standing by my side as I watch the interaction between the two friends. I feel a coldness on my hand and look down. Cassie has her hand in mine. I look back up, and her face shows concern.

"What can I do? No one will believe me if I tell them, Cass."

Before I can say anything else, I hear a

shriek, and one of the men has disappeared. The other is standing alone, gun raised to the night. I can see his whole body shaking.

I'm jolted back to reality by Kyle shaking me.

"It's gonna happen again. Some parents. They're going out there to stop whatever it is."

"Babe, calm down. You were dreaming."

"I know it was a dream. But two men are going out there. They won't make it out."

Kyle pulls me closer to him, trying to calm me down. "Shh. Just breathe. We'll talk about it in the morning. You just need to sleep some more."

I take a few deep breaths. Sleep isn't going to happen again tonight. I'm sure of that.

Chapter 7

I hate doctors' offices. They're cramped and impersonal and entirely too tidy for my liking. I like a little chaos in my décor.

Against my better judgment, Kyle has convinced me to go with him to a psychiatrist to talk about my dreams. He's promised that the lady will be nice, that she helped him through some childhood trauma years ago, and that, at the very least, it will be good for me to talk to someone other than him.

I'm not sure what good it will do. She has to keep everything she hears confidential, so if I tell her about Richard and Jason it won't do any good. No one will be warned; the two men will still go into the woods and die—soon. There was little time between dreams and reality lately, and I had a feeling that tomorrow morning there would be a new headline, more "breaking news" … only it wouldn't be news to me.

Kyle's arm is resting across my shoulders. My tight, rigid shoulders. Every muscle is tense, every joint locked and loaded for fight or flight. I really want to fly, Kyle or no. I'm tapping my fingers on the arm of the equally rigid chair, and one of my legs won't stop jumping. Up and down and up and down, the heel of my boot tapping against the carpeted floor. *Thump thump thump thump.* I bet the other couple in the waiting area—judging from his scowl and the terror in her eyes, probably here for marriage counseling—are annoyed with my foot by now.

"Katherine?"

I jump about ten feet high when my

full name is called. I had filled out the "preferred name" section of the form. Why is she using my full name, like I'm in trouble or something?

Kyle pulls me to my feet and puts a reassuring hand on the small of my back. I look up at Dr. Pamela Freeman, and my anxiety eases a smidge.

She's tall and pretty, middle-aged, with a pair of those cute little reading glasses balanced on the tip of her nose and a no-nonsense straight brown bob. Her pencil skirt is pressed and free of creases, though instead of a suit-type jacket she has a lightweight athletic jacket on, the kind that is supposed to wick away sweat while you're working out. I wonder for a moment if she's going to the gym after work. Something about the jacket calms me; I think if she had been wearing a suit jacket, I would've bolted.

"I-it's Kit, please," I say as I walk up to shake her hand. Kyle shakes hands with her as well, and they exchange pleasantries. She tries to tell Kyle to have a seat while the two of us go back, but I insist on him coming with. She nods in agreement before leading us down the hall to her office.

The actual office is more inviting than the waiting room. It's decorated in warm, calming shades of brown, and the infamous psychiatrist's couch is more like something from Ikea, all plush and cushy. I sit back into the cushion and breathe a small sigh of relief. Maybe this won't be too bad.

"So, Kit, what brings you in to see me today?"

I frown. "Didn't your receptionist give you the message?"

"Well, yes, but I like to hear from my patient. Messages are good for some things, but hearing directly from the source is always better, in my professional opinion." She gives me a little wink. "Besides, Meredith tells me that you have information on the recent Hunting Woods murders, and that definitely warrants a deeper, one-on-one conversation."

Meredith must be that young girl

behind the reception desk. She was nice when we checked in, but I wondered if she was laughing at me right now. I was honestly surprised she didn't laugh at me on the phone when I called in this morning. I swallow past a lump the size of Texas in my throat. Here it comes, I think. Here comes the part where I tell her my dead sister talks to me through music, and then she'll send me off to the psych ward. I take a deep breath and launch into my tale, from the night of the memorial to last night's dream. It all comes out in a rush of words, some stammered, some frantic, some a bit hysterical at the end.

Dr. Freeman is silent the whole time, her chin resting on her steepled fingers, with the occasional nod to acknowledge that I was talking. Her face is completely blank, and I don't know if that's a good sign or a bad sign.

I finish my tale and put my head in my hands. My shoulders are shaking from the release of all the pent-up stress, and Kyle rubs my back.

I have to give Kyle credit for being the awesome boyfriend that he is—even if he did take me to a shrink. He's never once said that I'm nuts for saying Cassie's talking to me through the music or for ranting on about my dreams, and he's been nothing but supportive ever since we first met.

It'll be a shame if they don't let him visit me in the psych ward.

The doctor remains quiet for a long time after I finish. Too long. Maybe she's trying to figure out if a straight jacket is necessary.

She picks up a pen and starts to take notes. I worry that she'll miss something important, that she'll forget a vital part of the story, but on the other hand I'm grateful she sat through the whole thing without interrupting or jotting down things like "paranoid delusions" or "schizophrenia."

"Dr. Freeman?"

She looks up from her notes, peering over her glasses to gaze directly into my eyes. I can't read her expression, and I'm getting scared. Sweat starts to bead on my forehead and trickle down between my shoulder blades.

After too long of a pause, she sits straight up and puts down her glasses. She leans back in her desk chair and taps the cap of her pen against the desk. "Kit, how long have you lived here?"

"My whole life. Why?"

She nods. "And have you heard the history of Hunting Woods?"

There's a history to Hunting Woods? "I might've skipped a class or two in school …"

She puts down her pen, neat and tidy next to her glasses. Everything in its place, I guess. "I don't think you did miss this class. I think you heard the stories in school, and after what happened to Cassie your conscious mind shut them out. Buried them. I think your subconscious mind is trying to remind you, and because of the tragedy, your mind is interpreting them as these nightmares."

I can feel my forehead getting that

stupid wrinkle it gets when I frown. Kyle thinks it's cute; I wish it would go away. "That doesn't explain why, when I turn on the news in the mornings, the very same thing has happened while I was sleeping—a day or two later, if I'm lucky."

"How much of these dreams do you remember when you wake up?"

"Everything. Every single detail."

Her eyes squint, just barely, just a little, but it's enough to make my heart sink in my chest. She doesn't believe me.

Before I can answer her, she sits forward a bit, pulls her keyboard closer, and starts tapping away at the keys.

Well, that's it. She's emailing the hospital right now, I bet.

After a few taps and clicks her printer starts to whir, and it spits out page after page after page. I start to worry that I'm going to get charged extra for ink and paper.

When it's done, she takes the sheets off the printer, taps them on the desk until they're neat and straight, and puts a staple in the top left corner at a perfect forty-five-degree angle. She hands me the packet.

"Read this. It's just the basics, but right here is a history of Hunting Woods." She taps a date on the top page. "It starts in the seventeen hundreds, but honestly I think there are oral accounts dating back farther, from the Native American tribes that used to live here. I think once you've read the stories again, after recent events, you'll see why you're getting the nightmares. That, combined with this prescription I'm writing for you, should stop them."

"It won't stop the murders," I mutter under my breath. Kyle jabs me in the rib with his elbow. "It won't!" I say again, a little too loud. I clamp my hands over my mouth, but the words are already out.

Dr. Freeman stands up and walks around her desk. She sits next to me on the couch and pats my knee. "I'm not saying this will work immediately, and I'm not saying it's a guarantee. But the pills — taken as directed — will put you in such a sleep that you shouldn't dream much, if any, and knowing the history will perhaps put your mind at ease a bit."

I glance down at the top page of the packet. It's a printout from a website, and there's a picture of an old, yellowed newspaper. The headline says, "Fifty Year Curse Strikes Again in Hunting Woods."

Tears well up in my eyes, and I try to blink them back. One stubborn tear gets through to run down my cheek and fall onto the paper. It lands on the word "Curse."

* * *

I spend most of that evening pouring over the papers from Dr. Freeman. I don't care what she says, this wasn't taught to me in school. I would remember stories of a mysterious monster that lives in the woods, coming out every fifty years to feed. Hell, my granddad's still alive, and I swear he's never mentioned it.

Mom and Dad had Cass when they were in high school. Maybe that's why they suck as parents — they never got to grow up and learn how to be adults before they had to take care of a kid — but that makes them kinda too young, really, for the fifty-year thing.

That bothers me, too, almost as much as never hearing about it. Why, if it rests fifty years in between, is it back just three short years after killing Cassie and her friends? That doesn't make any sense.

Of course, what part of an invisible, untraceable monster makes any sense?

Kyle tries to get me to come to bed, but I wave him off, too distracted by what I'm reading. In every other generation, almost exactly fifty years after the last series of murders, there's a rash of fresh killings in Hunting Woods. Whatever it is that's doing this, it waits long enough that most people forget — or maybe they don't want to remember. Either way, it's changed its M.O., and I'm filled with a sudden compulsion to figure out why.

Over the course of my reading, I learn that the name "Hunting Woods" actually comes from some obscure Native American name that literally translates to "the Hunter's trees." Like, whatever this "Hunter" is, those are *its* trees, and we're trespassing.

I hear gentle snoring from the bed, and the corners of my lips curl up into a little smirk. He refuses to admit that he snores, but I find it adorable. It's not that gross, snorting kind of snore that you see on TV. It's gentle, soft, even ... relaxing. It's the kind of snore I could sleep next to forever. If I could trust myself to go back to sleep, that is.

Monster, demon, hellhound — there are a whole slew of names for the supposed Hunter, and none of them are pretty. Couldn't one of the names be "fluffy huggy bunny-kins" or something?

I lose track of time, and before I know it the sun's peeking through the cheap apartment blinds. I remember that I promised Kyle I'd go looking for a new job today, and that means a shower at the very least, maybe some makeup to cover up the bags that I'm sure I have under my eyes from lack of sleep. I drag my messenger bag over to me by the strap and dig through the assortment of crap inside before finally finding a pen and an old receipt. I scribble a few things on the back of it while they're fresh in my mind:

-Granddad
-Indians
-library
-coffee

I pick up my cell and press my granddad's picture. It's early, but I'm pretty sure he'll be up, anyway. He likes to take morning walks in the mall, to check out old ladies who are doing their mall-walking, so he can hit on "the fit chicks."

The phone rings twice before he picks up. "Hey, pumpkin. How's my little girl today?"

I take a deep breath before I answer. "Granddad? I need to ask you about the woods …"

Chapter 8

"Can you tell me about this?" I drop some papers on the table in front of my granddad. It's everything I could find online, printed out.

He refused to talk to me over the phone, made me drive to his place. I convinced myself it was just because he misses me and wants the company, however, I heard fear in his voice. Always so strong and raspy, it turned soft and wavered when he heard the words "Hunting Woods."

He scans through the pages, his hands

shaking. His grey hair gives away his age more then the wrinkles on his face. His pale blue eyes seem to have lost the sparkle they once held. For the first time in my life, Granddad looks old, and it's sobering. I refuse to be deterred by sympathy, though; I'm glaring at him, waiting for something, an answer, anything.

"Don't go messing in those woods, kiddo. I don't want to lose you, too." He glances at me from across the table. "Promise me you'll stay out of them."

"Granddad, I don't plan on dying in some wooded area alone. I just—I want to know what happened to my sister. Why does this say it happens every fifty years, but nothing has been done to end it? And why is it happening again if it hasn't been fifty years?" The words spill out of me so fast, I can't stop myself. I have so many questions, and I need the answers now.

"Hey, kiddo. Just slow down." He puts his hand on mine. The warmth calms me a little. "Breathe. Getting upset won't help anyone."

"I'm having these dreams Granddad, and they're getting worse. I can't talk to anyone about it because they'll think I'm crazy. Cassie is trying to communicate with me. She's showing me things, and I need to understand what it all means if I'm going to be able to stop it."

He stares into my eyes, concern written on his face in the drawn brows, the slight frown, that damn wrinkle between the brows that I'm sure now is genetic. "Are you sure you're ready for this? It's a lot to take in."

"I already feel like I'm losing my mind, Granddad. I just need some answers. Maybe we can stop it." I squeeze his hand. "Maybe Cassie's death can be something more than just … forgotten. Maybe it can mean something."

He lets out a long sigh. "I'll tell you what I know. I'll even show you everything I've found. I want you to leave it at that though, love. You have a long life ahead of you. Don't mess it up with this."

I agree with him, for now, anyway.

"I believe it's something like a soul eater." My granddad spoke with a waver to his voice, a shuddering like the room had gone twenty degrees cooler in a heartbeat.

"What's a soul eater?" I ask.

"There are different stories about soul eaters; it always depends on the culture. Different versions of what they do or how they look. I believe this one nests in our woods. He slaughters a human and takes their soul to his nest, where he torments them until they are depleted. He steals their energy, and they become a part of him."

"So he has Cassie's soul? Could that be what she's trying to tell me, Granddad? How long does this torture last? She's not still suffering, is she?" The thought of her being tortured in the afterlife makes me angry. She didn't deserve that. Cassie was a good person.

"I would be skeptical about this whole Cassie's-talking-to-you thing, kiddo. Soul eaters are relentless and brutal; they never leave a soul unclaimed." Granddad's reply stung, but he was quick to amend it. "However, I've learned anything is possible."

"I've learned to be more accepting of odd and unusual things as well. This whole situation's been horrible." There's a long, uncomfortable silence between us before I start speaking again. "So, this thing is supposed to return every fifty years. Why is it back now? It's, like, forty-seven years too early."

I see my granddad thinking about the proper way to answer. I'm not sure he even has the answer. His eyes are sunken in, the sorrow weighing on him.

"If you look further, really dig, you'll find it never really leaves. It travels to different areas. It moves in a circle. I've spent years tracking this thing, but I never told anyone. I didn't want them to think I was losing it. It's backtracked. I don't know why." A long sigh escapes his lungs, and his face grows pale. He straightens and sets his shoulders. "Follow me."

Granddad stands up and grips his cane as he walks towards the basement door. He's leaning on it a little more than usual.

I look at the basement door with trepidation. The basement we were never allowed in when we were growing up. The basement that's always locked. He pulls a small set of keys out of his pocket and proceeds to open the door. I follow him down the narrow stairs, and he pulls the string in the middle of the room to turn on a single bulb.

The light is dim but illuminates the room just enough for me to see the chaos hanging on the walls. A huge map of the United States covers the right side of the room, tacks in the wall showing exactly where he's tracked this thing. On the left-hand side are hand-drawn pictures, newspaper articles, and handwritten notes from my granddad.

This beast, or demon, came to life in those drawings. The nightmares come flooding back, mocking me as I stared at the disfigured form. I shiver and try to ignore the images running through my mind. Through the dreams, I've seen this monster, felt its claws rending my flesh, smelled its rancid breath.

"How do you know what this thing looks like, Gramps? You have the image I've been seeing almost perfect."

"It's a long story, kiddo, but no one's ever escaped from this thing. No one except for me."

My jaw drops as he reveals his secret. He's beside me, staring at the map on the wall, off in his own world now. Maybe thinking about what happened to him, or maybe thinking about the same thing happening to Cassie.

"Granddad, what happened? You're saying you've seen this thing in person?"

"We'd just had our first snowfall of the year. Some of my buddies and I decided to go hunting. The deer were out, so it was the perfect time. We followed the tracks deeper into the woods. We didn't find the deer, but this thing found us. It took out all of my friends." His voice is thick with emotion, and I think about what it must be like, being the only survivor in an attack that brutal.

"How did you make it out?"

"I was lucky, that's how." He sits down at the table in the middle of the room and pats the chair next to him. "He had me. I thought I was dead. I could feel his claws digging into me. It was as if this thing was sucking the life out of me. I could see myself leaving my body. And then I heard voices, people calling out our names. It disappeared as quickly as it appeared. I woke up in the hospital. When I tried to describe what happened they put me in an institution. After a few months, I told them I imagined it all, and it was just an animal. I couldn't stay there anymore."

"Are there — do you have scars from it?"

Granddad laughs. "Kiddo, have you ever wondered why I use a cane? Your parents had your sister young; just because I'm a grandfather doesn't mean I'm ancient." He pulls up the leg of his Bermuda shorts to reveal a road map of thick white scars. Then he lifts the hem of his shirt, and I see just how close he came to death. I've seen pictures of burn victims with less scarring than this. The wounds he received at the — talons? Hands? What are they, exactly? — of the soul eater had been devastating. One scar in particular looks like his heart should have been torn in half by the wound, and I'm amazed that the surgeons back then were able to piece him back together again.

"I have so many questions for you right now, Gramps. I don't even know where to start. This is massive. People need to know."

"Little girl, people don't want to know. That's the issue. They want to ignore what's right in front of their eyes because it's easier not to believe. And you better not run off into those woods trying to be some kind of hero, because you can't get rid of it. It's a monster from Hell I tell you. It will take your soul back with it."

"Does anyone else know about this?"

I have a million questions coming to my mind. "Why didn't you say anything when Cassie—" My voice catches in my throat as I realize that Granddad knew what happened to Cass the whole time—and did nothing about it.

"There's nothing I could have said to change what happened to your sister. I told you, no one wants to know. It's easier for them that way."

"So we're just expected to sit back and let this thing continue to kill people? That's not right! There has to be something somewhere about how to get rid of it. We can't let it torture Cassie until nothing is left of her."

"I don't want that either, kiddo. However, I won't risk you or anyone else. Just stay away. That's the best thing you can do." His chair scrapes against the floor as he pushes back from the table to stand.

"Do you mind if I stay here for a while and go through all of this stuff you've gathered?"

"I'm getting tired. I'm going to go

back upstairs. You can hang out and look through my papers, though. At least, I know where you are then, and that you're safe."

I watch as he makes his way up the stairs, and when he is completely out of view, I turn my sights back to all the newspaper clippings and notes in front of me. This could take a while. Lucky for me, he seems to be very organized.

I pull my laptop out of my bag and set it on the table. Google will make this a whole lot easier. I pick up the first note. The handwriting is bit sloppy, but I make out the date and town. Names of people who were killed in the same fashion. I begin to put that info into the computer to see what else I can find out.

As the results pop up, I make a call to Kyle.

"Hey babe, you home yet?" His voice is a little frantic, and I wonder how long I've been here for him to be so concerned.

"I may be a while. This thing is fucking huge. I can't believe it's been buried. You should stop by when the band finishes practicing. You won't believe this shit, Kyle."

"Give me an hour, and I'll be there."

He hangs up, and I begin clicking on various articles. My head's already starting to hurt with all the information. The speakers of the laptop come to life, and *When Will Tomorrow Come* starts to play.

"I promise I'm going to figure this out, Cassie. Just give me some time."

Chapter 9

Granddad's notes lead me down a rabbit hole of demons, failed exorcisms, and more death than I care to think about.

Kyle joins me in the basement after band practice, and he pours over the info with me. "Damn, babe, no wonder you were kicking my ass in your sleep. If I was dreaming about this, this — fuck, I don't know what to call it! — I'd beat someone up trying to get away, too."

"Sorry again about that," I say. He's still got some lingering scratch marks and bruising from the last time we spent the night together in bed.

He takes my hand and gives it a squeeze. "No need to apologize, Kit. I know you can't control it when you're asleep."

"I'm starting to think I can't control anything, even awake." I put my head in my hands and sigh. "I'm hearing the music more often now. So often that I wonder if it isn't all my imagination. I mean, most of the time it's just me that's there when the music comes on. Maybe it's wishful thinking that Cass is trying to communicate with me more than anything."

"It's not, Kit." He rubs my back, a reassuring, anchoring touch in a life gone haywire. "I've heard it too, remember? So that part is one hundred percent, without-a-doubt not imaginary." He paused. "I can't interpret the songs like you can, though. You knew Cass better than anyone. You're her voice right now."

Tears brim in my eyes, and I try to blink them away. I'm only successful in causing them to spring forth, a cascade of fear and sorrow running down my face. "Oh, Kyle, I don't know what to do. This is so much bigger than me, this thing here. There are priests and hunters and medicine men that have tried to stop this thing, to kill or exorcise the soul eater, and none of them succeeded. I'm no monster hunter, and I'm no priest, that's for damn sure. How can I help Cassie when I'm just one woman against a demon that's hundreds, if not thousands, of years old?"

"I don't know — yet. But we'll find out together, and we'll save your sister's soul."

Kyle's support gives me hope even though the situation seems hopeless. I turn over the page I'm looking at and see something scrawled in different handwriting from Granddad's. I squint and hold it closer. It looks almost like song lyrics.

Fifty years, he makes his rounds
Fifty years, the screams resound
Fifty years 'til he returns
Fifty years with blood is earned

But if the demon tastes the song
He will not venture far or long
For the song, he stays nearby
Watching with his demon eye
For when the song's blood ripens sweet
Soon again the demon eats
If you be song, then stay away
Unless the sun's rays light your way

"Kyle, look at this," I say as I hand him the crumpled paper. "What the fuck do you think this means? You can't taste a song; it makes no sense."

He reads the note, tapping out a beat with a pencil eraser on the top of the desk. It's primal and frantic and fits the words perfectly. "I dunno, but it would make a kick-ass video. Dixie Piss could go viral with this."

"That's not funny." I yank the paper out of his hand and read it again. "I feel like this could be important, but I just don't understand it."

"Is Cass offering any advice?"

I pause to listen then shake my head. "Nope. Literally radio silence right now. I don't hear any music playing. Do you?"

"Just the beat I'm composing to this poem or whatever it is here."

I shove his shoulder and glare. "That's not funny, either. This is serious." I try to think of what the words in the song or poem could mean. "So, let's look at this. Fifty years is how long between this thing's murder sprees, so I get that part of it. But tasting the song? What does a song taste like?"

Kyle shrugs. "Maybe demons have different taste buds. Maybe songs do have a taste, to them at least."

"Hmm." I think about that for a moment. Cassie had her iPod with her when she died. Did the soul eater taste the music that was playing? Was that why she died?

No, that doesn't make any sense. None of the other victims had been listening to music or even were musicians. So what is the connection?

I try typing the words into the search engine, but no hits come up. I try searching "soul eater song" and "demon music eater" and even "songs about demons." A lot of hits on the last one, but nothing that fits our situation. As far as the Internet is concerned, there's no information anywhere on a soul-eating, song-eating demon.

A few minutes later, the door to the basement creaks open. "Kiddo? You guys hungry down there? It's dinner time."

Have we really been here all day? I glance at the time in the bottom corner of my screen and blink until my eyes clear and it comes into focus. Almost eight o'clock. Wow. We kept working right up until sundown.

"Yeah, Granddad, be right up!" The door closes without a reply, but I assume he hears me because I hear pots and pans clattering in the kitchen upstairs. "Hey, babe, you don't mind if we eat here tonight do you?"

Kyle leans back in his chair with his hands behind his head. "And turn down free food? Never."

I grab the back of his chair before he tips over. "Careful! Trust me, concussions aren't fun."

"Did your grandpa forget he was cooking?"

"Huh?"

He points to the basement steps, towards the door. "It just got really quiet up there."

I stand up and creep to the bottom of the steps. "Granddad?" I call out.

There's no answer.

"Granddad?" I climb up a few steps. Kyle is right at my heels, his hand on my shoulder. "Granddad, what's for dinner?"

Silence … until—

—The laptop's speakers start blasting out a song from Kyle's band that, to my knowledge, hasn't been recorded yet: *The Killer's in the House*.

I sprint up the stairs and burst through the basement door into the kitchen. The scene before me is straight from my nightmares, and I retch until my stomach's empty. I have to give Kyle credit for holding in his lunch, and for having the presence of mind to hold my hair back for me. Hot tears stream down my cheeks as I look at what's left of my granddad.

The room is littered with body parts and splattered with blood. Granddad's cane is in pieces, the handle clenched in his hands, as though he had fought back. Across the room, his face is frozen in a mask of terror, with deep gashes through his cheeks. I can see his teeth through the shredded skin.

"It-it's supposed to stay in the woods," I say, my voice small and shaky. "We're not in the woods. Why'd it come out of the woods?"

Kyle holds me close. "It travels around. Maybe the woods aren't a good enough hunting ground anymore?"

"Granddad ..." Shock sets in. I'm shaking all over, and nothing seems real.

"Sit down." Kyle guides me to the dining table, which remains blood-free. He kneels next to the closest smear of blood on the kitchen floor. "How did we not hear this happening? There was no screaming, no shouts, not a sound."

"It-it got him, Kyle. It got him when he was young, and it came back and finished him off."

He squints and leans closer. "There's something written in the blood here."

"W-what d-does it s-s-say?" My teeth are chattering. It feels like the temperature has dropped thirty degrees despite the pot of water boiling over on the stove.

"I almost didn't see it; it's not English. I don't even know for sure that it's letters, but it's definitely not random." He takes his phone out and takes a bunch of pictures from different angles, careful not to step in Granddad's remains. He looks up from what he's doing, and sorrow fills his eyes even though he'd only just met Granddad. "Kit, we're going to have to clean this up. If we call the cops, they'll think we did this. This thing, this soul eater, leaves no evidence. No fingerprints, no footprints. Everything will point to us. Can you do that, Kit?"

I shake my head and pull my knees up to my chest. "I can't do that. Not with Granddad."

Kyle nods. "Okay. I'll get it. I'll take

care of it. You can — is there a place you can go lie down? I don't want you passing out on me and falling out of that chair."

I let him lead me into Granddad's guest room — I can't stand the thought of trying to lie down in his own bed right now — and curl up into a ball on the guest bed. Kyle sets to task cleaning up the kitchen.

I cry until my eyes throb and my throat feels like it's going to close. I cry until there's nothing left, until my lids grow heavy, and thought I try to fight it, I find myself drifting off to sleep ... where the nightmare, the soul eater, waits for me ...

Hunting Woods is quiet — too quiet. No birds chirping, no leaves rustling. Dead silence.

I look around, and I get that feeling where I'm me-but-not-me. I feel like I'm not in the present, like today hasn't happened yet. "Cassie?" I call out, and I wonder why I say that name. It's not one I know. Or do I?

No one answers, but I'm not surprised. There's no one here, after all. Just me, and what's left of my friends.

That's right! I was running for my life. My friends are dead, and I'm not far behind them if I don't run.

Where did it go? It was right behind me. It is right behind me. I can feel its hot breath on my neck. I wheel around, but I see nothing. I hear nothing. The woods are thick with the stench of death, though; that much prevails.

I take a step, and I wonder why my leg burns until I look down and see the blood seeping through my jeans — or rather, what's left of my jeans.

I'm dead if I don't stop.

I take another step, and another, and another, fighting against the searing pain in my leg. I round a copse of trees, and there it is. The thing, the thing that killed my friends and hunts me now.

"What do you want?"

The monster's mouth gapes, and if this thing was a person, I'd swear it was smiling. It stands there, bloody saliva oozing from its teeth, and though the jaw doesn't move I hear its voice echo in my head.

"You are close, but you are not the one I seek. The one who will sustain me through

eternity."

"What does that mea — "

Before I can finish, it lashes out. Razor-sharp claws shred the flesh of my chest, missing my heart and lungs but incapacitating me nonetheless. I fall to the ground, and the last thing I hear before the search and rescue dog's howl is the rasping laughter of the monster as it fades away.

Chapter 10

The bodies of two men were found in Hunting woods yesterday afternoon by park rangers who were making their daily rounds. Ranger McCord said not much was left of the victims who appeared to be torn apart.

The rifles found by the remains were traced back to identify the men as Brendon Yearling (42) and Calvin Hurst (40). They were found on a small path near Hunting Lake.

Reports from the rangers say that

the two men could've been attacked by a wild animal, or a pack. No further information has been released at this time. Rangers and city police still advise everyone to stay out of the woods until they can capture the animal responsible for these deaths.

I see a picture of the two men to the right side of the short article. Both men are clean cut in the photo. They were the same men in my dream the other night. They were out there trying to find this thing, having no idea what they were really up against. All they wanted was to protect the kids of the town, their kids.

And once again, Cassie was right. If there was only a way I could've warned them without sounding crazy. How do you approach someone with something like that anyways? No matter what, you end up sounding like a complete nutcase. It wouldn't have changed anything.

My eyes hurt from staring at the computer screen. I've been sitting here since I first woke up at seven this morning, trying to find more information.

I thought I could find something my granddad had missed in his own research. Hours spent, only to find nothing new at all. It seems my granddad was very thorough when he was researching this himself. I'm sure my few hours are nothing compared to the hours, the years he put in, the time he spent traveling to these places.

Granddad's funeral was yesterday. Closed casket, of course. Thanks to Kyle's cleanup efforts, the cops didn't know we had been in his house when he was killed. We called it in but claimed we had just arrived to find him — what was left of him — in the kitchen. Mom and Dad rushed the paperwork to take care of his things. The estate auction is in a few days, but since he owned his house outright, Mom said I can take it. It takes some of the burden off me as far as housing goes, because I still haven't found a job after the record store closed. I'll have to move my stuff in eventually, though, move back into the place where Granddad was slaughtered.

All of this thinking just makes me miss Cassie even more. However, I'm starting to hate it when she does show up because I know what that means. It means something's about to happen. Usually, that something isn't good.

I raise my hand up to my eyes and wipe, trying to get rid of the stinging sensation, only making it worse than it was. My cheeks are hot and damp from all the crying I've done throughout the day. I try to push on, though, looking for anything at all on this creature, trying new keywords in the search bar, anything at all that will help me understand why this thing is killing people. Why it's slowly taking out members of my family. I can't seem to pull up even half of the information my grandfather had found. All I really know is this: I have to put an end to it. I can't lose anyone else.

I consider myself a strong person, but all of this makes me feel so helpless. With Cassie trying to tell me something and now Granddad being gone, it feels like my life's falling apart, and I have no idea how to fix any of it. Everything I think I find just leads to another dead end. There's nothing more in my search. Just stories of deaths in wooded areas. It's as if no one, other than my gramps, has even connected the attacks with each other. He definitely was on to something. And I know I now have to finish his work and figure it out, even if it kills me. This is going to end. I will make sure of that.

I lean back in my chair for a moment and wipe my eyes for what has to be the millionth time. When I look back at the screen, the page changes on its own. I've learned over the past few years when something like that happens, to just let it go. I know it means Cassie is beginning to guide me. It appears to be an old newspaper article from the Heritage Reservation that sits right outside of the woods to the north.

FOUR MEN ENTER THE WOODS, ONLY ONE RETURNS

The headline alone grabs my unwavering attention. I needed something to wake me up. I was beginning to feel like I was drowning in dead ends, and processing words was starting to fail me. I begin to read the article.

Four young men decided to spend an evening in the woods yesterday, hunting, before the first snowfall of the year. Things did not go as planned, however; only one of them made it out of the woods by crawling to a nearby post.

He's currently in the Riverbend hospital ICU recovering from wounds inflicted by what he called a pale white demon.

Two-Feathers, the sole survivor of the group, claims that they were attacked by a demon monster while tracking a deer in the woods. His tale, almost too farfetched to believe, has raised a few eyebrows amongst the reservation police. Tribal police are currently investigating the scene and will provide more details when the investigation is complete.

There's a picture of a boy, young man as the paper called him, lying in a hospital bed. His eyes were wide and wild. Fear. You could see the fear. Poor guy. I feel sorry for him. Before I can finish my thoughts, the page turns again.

"Cassie, this better be leading to something. I'm getting pretty tired of reading," I say out loud, speaking more to myself than to her. The computer shuts off, and the lights begin to flicker.

"Come on, Cassie. I'm not trying to be rude. I've just been at this all day. My eyes hurt. I need a break."

The room's silent and black. I hear the door rattle a little and then open. My heart sinks, and I feel the hair on the back of my neck stand up. A light breeze rushes through the door. Unexplained terror falls upon me.

"Hey, why are you sitting in the dark, babe?"

Kyle. I take a deep breath and exhale. I see a shadow in the door frame, and it begins to move into the room.

"I think I upset Cassie, and she shut off the power." I tap my fingers on the table, hoping that will get her attention, so she returns the electricity to working.

"Wow, she must be getting stronger if she can do that."

"I've spent all day researching stuff, and I told her I was getting tired. Then everything just went black."

I hear him laugh in the darkness as his footsteps get closer to the table where I'm sitting. "She's young; just imagine how powerful she can be. Your encouragement and willingness to communicate with her just helps her."

Terror surges back as the wrongness of the conversation registers in my mind. The scent, the sound, it's all Kyle. However, the words aren't his. The door slams, and I jump. Another gust of air sweeps the room, and I can see eyes glowing.

"W-what the f-f-fuck are you?" I stammer while trying to get the words out of my mouth.

I'm knocked out of my chair and to the ground. It's on my chest, pushing down on my sternum, making it hard to get air. I gasp, my hands clawing at the monster. I can hear it speaking to me, but its mouth doesn't move.

"I took her life, but her soul got away from me. I want her back. I don't lose souls."

"Cassie, help me!" I scream into the darkness.

My arms flail around, trying to fight off the monster that's holding me down. His claws dig into my chest, and I feel warm dampness seep out of my skin. The pain spreads as he rips his claws down. I close my eyes. When I open them again, Kyle is on top of me, trying to hold my arms down.

"Babe, calm down. It's me. Stop fighting!" Kyle's nose gushes blood, and his eye is bright red.

"It was here. It came in the door and sounded like you. The room was dark, I couldn't see, but it sounded just like you."

"What are you talking about? We need to get you to the doctor. You're bleeding pretty bad, babe. How did you cut yourself?"

"I didn't do this, Kyle. The creature,

monster, soul eater … whatever the fuck you want to call it. It was here. I think it's looking for Cassie. I don't know why; it was confusing."

Kyle scoops me up and rushes me to the car, the whole time holding a towel tight to my chest area. He places me in the car and rushes around to the other side.

Several hours and forty stitches later, I'm sitting in a hospital bed, trying to be calm and explain to Kyle everything that happened. His face remains blank the whole time, though. Like he isn't there at all.

Chapter 11

I thought I'd be released as soon as I was stitched up, but I'm still here. In this stupid hospital bed, hooked up to these stupid monitors. The *beep-beep-beep* is annoying. I mean, I know it means my heart's still working, but—couldn't they find a better sound?

Dr. Freeman shows up a little after five-thirty. They must've called her when I was admitted. I wonder if my insurance will cover a hospital consultation. I doubt it. How am I supposed to pay for all this shit?

She talks with me for an hour about my dreams, about what I'd found out about the soul eater, about my granddad. I don't tell her what happened to him. I know that her confidentiality goes out the window if murder is involved, and if I tried to tell her what really happened, she'd just chalk it up to a psychotic break and have me committed. Or arrested. Or both.

She excuses herself to talk to the nurse, but I'm already pretty sure she's ordering some kind of sedative or antipsychotic or something. I guess if it gets rid of the dreams, I'll take it. Anything's gotta be better than these nightmares.

Kyle shows up after she leaves with some coffee and brownies. I know damn good and well he didn't get those brownies at the cafeteria, and I gobble them up. Since the nurse hasn't brought whatever Dr. Freeman ordered yet, I might as well do some self-medicating.

"Sorry I was distant, babe," he says as

I wipe brownie crumbs from my lips. "You just scared the shit out of me, and I'm having a real hard time wrapping my mind around the possibility that you didn't do this to yourself, especially when you've attacked me in your sleep before."

I see tears form in his eyes, and I feel kinda bad about it.

"I just don't want anything to happen to you. With what happened to Cassie and now your grandpa — I don't want you to be next." He rakes a hand through his hair. His head hangs down, and he's looking up at me through his thick lashes. "Kit, babe, I really think we need to leave. Get the fuck outta Dodge. Maybe if we leave, it won't find you again. All the old stories say that it moves around, yeah, but it has a pattern — a hunting ground, if you will. Maybe we just need to get far enough away that it won't come after you."

I feel the muscles in my face harden, and I bite my tongue. He wants me to leave Cass behind? I can't do that. I should say something. Argue. Try to get this crazy idea out of his head. Why am I not saying anything?

"Kit?"

I'm still not saying anything. I try to find words, but I'm just so tired of trying to explain myself.

After a long pause, he sighs and stands up. "All right. Fine. Stay. Stay and get murdered. I'm done, Kit. Done with this whole mess. I can't keep watching you go through all this, seeing you hurt and scared. It's killing me to see you suffering like this."

My jaw drops, and I'm shaking. I'm trying to wrap my mind around the words coming out of Kyle's mouth, to make sense of it, but I can't. Would he really leave me now, when I need him most?

He crosses the room and brushes a lock of hair out of my face. I close my eyes, and a fat tear runs down my cheek. He wipes it away and places a soft kiss on my forehead. "Take care, Kit. Be safe. And whatever you do, stay away from Hunting Woods."

When I open my eyes, he's gone.

The nurse comes in with a medicine cup of pills and some water. I take the pills without asking what they're for. Who cares anymore? Life's just one big shit show, anyway.

I drift through the next couple of days without really taking anything in. I sleep, I eat, I lie in the hospital bed waiting for Kyle to realize that he's wrong, to come back and apologize for leaving me there.

By the time I'm discharged, he still hasn't returned.

It takes me a while to find where he parked my car. I suppose I should be grateful he left it; otherwise, I'd have to take a cab home.

The drive home is longer than usual without Kyle there to talk to. I turn on the radio to drown out the silence, but it's a song that reminds me of him, so I turn it back off. Cassie is conspicuously absent. The radio doesn't come to life to play me a song of heartache and loneliness, and I'm wondering if she's mad at me, too.

I get home, half expecting Kyle to be

waiting for me, but the apartment is empty. Just furniture and clothes and stuff—no Kyle. Upon closer inspection, my heart sinks. Yes, there are clothes here, but they're all mine. Kyle's stuff is all gone—everything except the cool drumsticks I got him for his birthday last year. Those are sitting on the bed, as lonely as I am.

He really left me.

I want to be mad at him. I want to hate him for leaving me during all this shit. But I can't. Much as I hate to admit it, he was right. I should make myself a ghost before the soul eater turns me into one for real. Why am I still here?

I know the answer: Cassie.

I don't want to leave her. Don't want to abandon this town and the only chance at saving her soul, if her soul's still there to save.

Cass isn't Kyle's responsibility, but she is mine. He can get out, get safe, but I can't. Not while I can still do some good. This realization steels me, gives me purpose, and I square my shoulders and set my jaw. I have a responsibility. I have to do something to save Cass. If I just buckle down and focus, maybe I can find something Granddad couldn't, some way to stop the soul eater.

I fall asleep clutching the drumsticks, the cursor on my laptop flashing where I left off with my notes.

Survivors: Granddad, Two-Feathers
Victims: Holy fuckballs, it's a lot
Clues: Tasty songs? Fifty years, don't go in the woods, something about the sun?
Ideas: |

Chapter 12

Kyle

I turn my ear towards the trees and squat next to the path leading into the woods, holding my breath. Listening closely, trying to take in all of the sounds of the forest ... only there are no sounds, no noises, not even the chirp of crickets. The air is still; no breeze blows through the leaves. No animals rustle in the overgrowth. Nothing. All I hear is the loud thumping of my heart in my chest. It reminds me of the drumbeat of a song I wrote a while back.

I've got three days. Three days until a few idiots in town decide to go out and play in the woods, just for fun. And I can't tell them how dangerous it is because that's what's luring them out there. They *want* to court the danger. There would be no stopping Kit from trying to go out and save them, either. That's why I have to stop this shit before she gets hurt again.

I walk back to the van and grab a pack of smokes. I'm not sure if I'm ready for this, but I have no choice. I have to risk it. Have to fight that *thing* that's out there.

A light flickers in the darkness as I flick my Bic, and I bring the flame up to the cigarette. "I'm coming for you, bastard! Do you hear me?" I shout into the void, not knowing if anyone—or anything—can hear me. I take a long drag from the cigarette and toss the butt to the ground, grinding it out with the heel of my shoe. I take out my phone and steel myself for what I'm about to do.

I pull up my messenger app and finds

Kit's name.

Kit,

I never wanted to hurt you. Someone needs to stop this craziness though, and I have a plan. If everything goes right I'll be back for you, if you'll have me back. If not, know I love you, and I'll always be around in some way.

I read the message back. I want to say more, but I can't find the words. Why is it so hard to say the right thing? I hit send and toss the phone back in the van. Pulling out another cigarette, I light it and take a long puff, looking up into the night sky. "It's now or never."

I head down the path into the woods, taking out the gun I stole from my deadbeat dad. I check the safety, making sure it's off before I venture too far in.

You never know what's out there. Better to be sure.

My feet seem to find every damn dry twig and branch in the woods. At first, I try to move slowly and quietly, but that goes out the fucking window as the underbrush snaps and cracks. Whatever this thing is out there, it's already heard me by now.

I keep my finger on the trigger. The second I see anything, even a flash, I'll fire. Dad, for what he's worth, taught me how to use the gun when I was a kid. I haven't fired one in years, but it's not too hard. Aim. Squeeze. Done.

If I can just find the bastard, I can save Kit. It's not much, but it's something to hope for.

The cigarette dangles from my lips as I stalk through the forest, its red tip glowing with every inhale. I scan the darkness between the tree trunks, but I don't see anything.

An hour passes without any sign of the thing that killed Kit's granddad.

I don't understand it. Does the thing know I have a gun? It didn't stop it from slaughtering those two dudes who went in after it. I can't imagine this thing would be scared of a gun, but at the same time, it has to know I'm after it. Maybe it's hiding.

I've almost circled back to the parking lot when I hear a *snap* that didn't come from me. I freeze, gun held level, and swivel in place, eyes peeled for anything weird.

I don't see anything.

Not until the claws appear in my chest.

I choke on blood as I look down at the long, spindly things protruding from my shirt. They're not human fingernails, not animal claws, not anything I can identify. A dry, raspy laugh echoes in my ear as the thing pulls them back out. Spurts of blood pump from the wounds, and I drop to my knees.

It got me. The fucker got me.

A shadowy figure circles around me, eyes glowing in the pitch-black night. My hand shakes as I raise the gun, aiming at the glow. I pop off three shots before the claws lash out and slash my throat. I drop the gun and try to staunch the blood, but even as I do it, I know it's too late.

Long, jagged teeth appear in a crooked smile in front of me. *"You are not*

the song," it says.
Then everything goes black.

Chapter 13

Kit

The morgue is cold and sterile. Goosebumps rise on my arms as my sandals echo in the room with each step. I'm wearing a sundress, and I feel absolutely ridiculous as I shiver in the air conditioning.

To my credit, I didn't know I'd be headed for the morgue when I got dressed this morning.

The cop escorting me takes my arm when I freeze at the edge of the metal table. "Are you sure you're up to this, miss?" he asks.

I nod and gesture at the coroner to go ahead.

He lifts the sheet off the body on the table, and a strangled sound escapes my throat as I recognize Kyle.

What's left of Kyle.

"Did — did he suffer?"

The coroner shakes his head. "From the looks of it, most of the wounds had very little bleeding. He was likely dead long before ... Well, before most of the damage was done."

I swallow back bile and nod, then look to the officer. "That's him. It's Kyle."

The officer nods, and the coroner replaces the sheet. "Thank you, miss. I'm sorry for your loss."

Such a stupid phrase. Why is he apologizing? He didn't kill Kyle.

Nothing human did this.

"Do you know what he was doing in the woods?" the officer asks.

I shrug and shake my head. There's no point in trying to explain. How can I?

I'll be carted upstairs to the psych ward if I try to tell them that Kyle was probably hunting a supernatural killer. A monster. "No. We'd just broken up. I had no idea he was out there."

"Did you know Kyle had a gun?"

That's news to me. "No. I think he mentioned his dad having one once, but they weren't close."

He jots something down in a little notebook, just like on TV. Go ahead. I promise that note about Kyle's dad having a gun won't help you find the killer. Try researching indigenous monsters or something instead.

The cop has a few more questions for me, but I honestly don't know anything. The message Kyle left on my phone is the only clue I have for him, and it's not much. All it proves is that Kyle planned on doing *something* in the woods last night. Not really the hard evidence I'm sure the cop is looking for.

I leave the hospital with a heavy heart. I was supposed to be job hunting this afternoon, but how can I now? Kyle's dead, and I'm all alone.

When I get back to the apartment, the lack of his belongings hits like a sack of bricks. I can't take it anymore. I scream and cry and throw stuff until it looks like the monster ransacked the place. When I've worn myself out, I sit in the middle of the chaos and sob.

It's time. Time to leave, time to pack up my shit and move into Granddad's place. I can't take this anymore. My life is turning into a never-ending bad memory. At least, Granddad's place doesn't have any happy memories to confuse me. Maybe that's what I need: a clean slate. A fresh start.

A fresh start with Granddad's research in the basement.

The cops searched his house, of course, but I guess nothing they found down there seemed important to them. They catalogued everything, sure, took photos, but when I click on the lights and head down the stairs after dumping my things in the foyer, it's like I had never left. All of Granddad's newspaper clippings, notes, and drawings are still there. A neat little timeline of terror.

Time loses all meaning. I don't know if I've been in the basement an hour or a week. I go upstairs to use the bathroom and force myself to eat, but besides that, I dive into his research like it's my only lifeline left.

Cassie's been silent lately. Too silent. It could be that even she's given up. The Pandora station plays totally random shit. Nothing helpful.

Nothing helpful, that is, until I find a phone number for Two-Feathers in my search.

As soon as the name and number pop up on my screen, the song changes mid-beat. Instead of a pop anthem, it's suddenly a dark, death-metal riff.

Deep inside/Dead inside
Darkness surge and/Darkness rise
Question not the fate of man
Question death that walks the land

Okay, Cass, that was creepy. "Death that walks the land"? What does that mean?

I click the tab for the Pandora window to see the name of the song, but the screen freezes. By the time I get it to refresh, the song has ended, and it's back to the regular station.

Not wanting to miss my chance, I jot down the contact info for Two-Feathers and type the numbers into my phone with a shaking hand.

It rings seven times before he answers. I'd almost given up, but something told me to wait. When he picks up, the voice that answers is eerie, empty ... dead.

"Hello?"

I clear my throat and steel myself for a difficult conversation. "Hello, Two-Feathers?"

"Yeah?"

"M-my name is Kit. You don't know me, but — but I know you. Well, I know of you. My grandfather was attacked, you see, by the same thing that I think attacked you. My sister, too. And I think it's after me."

I sound like a lunatic. I wait for a

response, and for a moment I think he's hung up on me.

"You're the song."

"I beg your pardon?"

Shuffling on the other end, like he's moving. "Only the song can escape it. Only the song can end it."

"Sir? Please, Two-Feathers, I need to know how you escaped. How you got away."

Dry laughter greets me on the other end. "Escape? No soul can escape it. Only the song. The song is the only soul strong enough to combat the beast."

"Sir, I don't understand. You escaped it; you got away."

"I did not escape. I lived. A life without a soul is no escape."

A life without a soul …?

Realization slams into me, and I drop my phone.

The empty voice … the dry, dead laugh … Two-Feathers may have lived through the monster's attack, but he didn't escape … he lost his soul.

Dear God, the thing took his soul and

left him alive.

I pick my phone back up. "Sir? How can the song stop it?"

More of that dry, dead laughter. "Only the song can stop it. Only the song can escape. The song has the power."

Once I realize he's ranting, I hang up.

That was useless. More crap about a song, but a song isn't a person. I can't be a song. What was he talking about?

I guess losing your soul makes you a bit crazy.

I sit back with a sigh and run my hands through my hair, getting caught on about seven tangles. Time for a shower.

When I stand up to go upstairs, a loud *thud* makes me jump. I turn around, and on the floor by a bookshelf is an old photo album. It landed open, so I walk over to see what pictures are there.

A school talent show photo from the 70s stares up at me, with a band of teens at the center. The lead singer looks familiar, but I can't quite place him at first. I look at the caption beneath, and for the first time something about this makes sense.

It's Granddad's band.

Granddad was a musician.

Like Kyle. Like Cassie would have been if she'd had a chance at life.

Like *I* might have been if Cass hadn't died.

Could the song not be a song? Could it mean a musician? What does music have to do with this monster, and how can I use it to stop him?

Chapter 14

I look at the GPS screen for what has to be the twentieth time. Ten more miles on this road. I swear to myself that it said the same thing last time I looked. The trip seems like it's taking forever, and I'm surrounded by nothing but trees with an occasional open field here and there. The houses are few and far between, and I haven't seen a wild animal anywhere, which I find strange.

I switch the song on the radio and turn the volume up to drown out the noise in my head just as the GPS comes to life, making me jump in the seat. My heart almost leaps out of my chest.

"In one quarter mile, take a right on Crow's Nest Road."

"Ya, sure. Thanks for the warning," I reply.

A tiny little path appears in between towering trees, a one lane dirt road that anyone would miss if they didn't know it was there. I come to a stop as I start to make the turn. There's a chain going across the road, a sign warning against trespassers. Maybe it's a sign just for me. Perhaps I should turn around and go home. Pack all my things, move across the country to be closer to my parents. Get away from this thing.

Trees loom over the small path, making things seem darker than they are, and a thick mist appears out of nowhere. Just like in the horror movies I watched with Cassie as a kid. I'm on high alert, expecting something to rush out of the woods at me. I get out of the car and walk over to one side of the road, releasing the chain so I can pass through.

I have to push an eerie feeling away and force myself to continue. I feel eyes on me as my car creeps down the little road. Something out in the distance, glaring at me. I know it's that thing. It seems to be getting closer and closer as time goes by, and I can't escape it.

"You better have some answers for me, Two-Feathers. I really need some help with this," I say as my eyes again scan the woods surrounding the road trying to see through the fog. You would think after getting attacked by that thing I would move away from wooded areas, not go deeper into the woods.

The path finally opens a bit, and I spot a small shack. There's an old pickup truck sitting in the front. Rust has eaten up the sides of it, and the thing looks unsafe to drive. As I come to a stop beside the truck, a crow lands on the hood of my car. A horrible sound escapes his beak. Not a caw. An earsplitting *scream*. I shudder and rethink what I am about to do. Maybe I should really move away. It wouldn't follow me, would it? Surely the monster would lose interest and move on if I disappeared. The bird screams at me again, and I turn my car off.

Of course, I'm going in. I can't run away from this thing. Even if I did escape it, how many more people would die? Something has to be done, and it seems like I am the only one willing to try. I swing the car door open and step out, taking in a deep breath and gathering all the courage I can. It feels like death in this place. The crow flies toward me, and I duck just in time. He swoops back down, and I run towards the shack. Before I reach the door, there's a crashing sound, and the scream of a child echoes from inside.

I stop running and stand near the old wooden door, listening. Utter silence. Did I imagine it? My skin crawls. I knock on the door. Nothing.

"I know someone's in there. I heard you just a minute ago." I can barely hear my own voice. It's shaky and small. I knock on the door again. The results are the same. I look at the ground, gathering courage. It's now or never, I think to myself.

"I'm opening the door," I shout as I turn the handle. The door creaks as I give a little push and let go of the metal knob, allowing the door to slowly swing open. A cold rush of air sweeps across me, and I step inside the dark room. My hand automatically reaches out to the wall and searches for a switch. It only takes a moment to find what I'm looking for, and the room is flooded with light.

My eyes go right to a figure lying on the floor in the middle of the trashed room, a pool of blood already forming around the still body. I kneel down beside the old man. He's indigenous by the looks of him — dark skin, long, straight nose, wiry white hair that still has threads of jet-black coursing through it. I found who I was looking for, but all too late. "Two-Feathers, I'm so sorry. If I got here earlier, perhaps I could have helped you."

There are deep gashes on the man's

bare chest, with matching white scars underneath. This isn't the first time it's gone after this man. I stare at the wounds, examining the layers of flesh, the exposed muscle and bone beneath. I see something white and think it's a rib until I lean closer in. A claw — it broke a claw off inside this poor man. I pull out my knife and try to dig the piece of nail out, but as I'm blade-deep inside of him his arm reaches out and grabs at me, catching my forearm in his hand.

I jump and stumble backwards, and the knife makes a clanking sound as it hits the floor beside him. He still has a tight grip on my arm as he gasps for air, putting me off balance. I manage to stay upright, but his pull makes it awkward.

"Oh my God, you're alive! Let me get something to put on your wounds."

"There's no time; it took my grandson." He sputters, a cough escapes him, and blood splatters on my face. "The damn thing took my grandson. He's only three. You have to save him."

It took a kid? But why? Aside from

the older teenagers like Cassie, it's never gone after children before, and never one this young. Besides, it doesn't take people, it shreds them.

"I don't know where he is. I don't know how to stop it…"

Two-Feathers coughs again, spewing more thick blood. "Y-you know it? You know of what I speak?"

"Well, yeah … Kinda. Look, you need a doctor—"

Fading eyes scan my face, as though searching for something. "You are different. Not like the others …"

"Hush. Let me find something to staunch the bleeding." There's gotta be a towel or something in all this mess … I scan the area, but don't see anything useful within reach. I'd get up to search, but Two-Feathers still has an iron grip on me.

As if things weren't weird enough, my phone blares to life, playing "Soothe the Savage" by Monkey Jeff.

Damnit, Cass. This isn't the time!

Two-Feathers blinks and looks at my

pocket. "The song …"

"Yeah, sorry. I swear, I didn't touch any buttons. I don't know why it does that." Okay, that's a lie. I know what — *who* — is doing it.

"I see now …" A raspy breath shudders through him. "I see the song."

How can you see a song? I'm so confused.

He lets go of my arm and fumbles on the floor next to him. His hand bumps into the knife I dropped, and he picks it up with clumsy fingers. "The song is in you; you have to bring it out. Only you…" His voice trails off, and his breathing becomes even more ragged.

"I don't understand! Look, just try to stay still. I'll call for help," I say as I lean in closer to his face. "I'll be back. I have to call the cops — call an ambulance."

"Please, just go find my grandson. Return him to his parents. That's how you can help me." His voice is shaking, and it takes everything I have in me to make out the words that come from his mouth. "The knife. Keep it close. You will need it. It's special. It's blessed."

"Wait! You recognize that knife?"

"The knife will release the song …" Another cough. More blood. "The song will kill the beast."

"I don't even know where to find the thing. I don't know where it took your grandson." Panic surges through me. This is too much. Too much shock, too much violence, too much death. It's too damn much for me. "How can I find your grandson if I can't even find the monster? It's always one step ahead of me and one step behind me. It's all around me, and I can't even find it."

"Calm…" His words trail off for a moment. A gurgling sound interrupts. "The woods … Hunting … deep … where no one goes … Lair … it's there. It's scared of you. You are the song, the light." His hand reaches out to me and then drops to the floor. The claw I'd been trying to dig out of him earlier rolls from his fingers into the pool of blood next to him.

"Two-Feathers? Two-Feathers!" I

shake his shoulders, but his head just lolls back and forth. No more words come strangled from his mouth, no more jagged breaths.

He's dead.

None of this makes sense. It doesn't make sense for the monster to kidnap a kid, doesn't make sense that Two-Feathers called me the song … none of it. I want to scream, but I'm just so tired. Deep in my soul, I'm exhausted. I feel like I haven't slept in years, like all it would take is a strong gust of wind to knock me over.

With Two-Feathers gone, I stop looking for something to stop the bleeding and switch to looking for a sheet to cover him. I guess I can give him that much dignity. I get up and start searching the mess.

When I come across a photo album, I stop to look through it. It's like opening a time capsule. Glossy images of an indigenous family smile up at me. I see Two-Feathers in many of the pictures, along with a young couple and their small child. It must be his grandson.

The more I peruse the pictures, the more guilty I feel. This poor kid! He must be terrified. I'm an adult, for Christ's sake, and I can barely function with all the horrors I've faced lately. I can't imagine a little kid having to deal with the monster, having to watch his grandfather ripped to shreds.

Fuck. So much for moving to Boston to hide with Mom and Dad. So much for chickening out. My conscience sees the goofy smile in these photos and screams at me to help.

Okay, what did Two-Feathers say? Something about a lair? I wrack my brain for anything I might remember about something like that in Hunting Woods, but I come up blank. Deep in the woods, where no one goes … I mean, there's the old, abandoned mining caves. They're condemned or something. Maybe the monster hides out there?

It's the only clue I have. I find a blanket and drag it over Two-Feathers' body, covering him. With the photo album in hand, I pick up my knife and wipe off the blood.

Better get moving. No telling how long his grandson has.

Chapter 15

I can't believe I'm heading back to Hunting Woods.

I should be doing whatever I can to get the fuck away from there. But no, now I'm driving straight for it.

I must be fucking crazy.

Even crazier than my suicidal tendencies is the way the world just keeps on going. It's like no one knows what danger they're in. People are just going about their daily lives, totally ignorant of what's lurking. I'm fighting the midday traffic on the way to my certain death, and no one in these other cars has a fucking clue.

Traffic thins out the closer I get to Hunting Woods. People aren't as stupid as I thought, I guess. They're avoiding the one place they should. Of course, the caution tape and warning signs put up by the rangers help a bit.

I get to the ranger station where they hold the annual memorial for Cass and the other kids and park my car. Scanning the parking lot, I see no other cars around. Not even a ranger vehicle. It's eerie, like an abandoned ghost town. The temperature's dropping too, likely caused by the fog that followed me from Two-Feathers' shack. I shiver as I get out of the car and dig a hoodie from the back, shoving Cass's destroyed iPod and the knife Kyle gave me in the pockets. I grab a map of Hunting Woods from the display of pamphlets outside the ranger station. A quick check shows that it has the old mining caves marked. They're marked as a restricted area, off-limits, but they're marked, and that's what I need.

The map goes in my pocket with the iPod, but not before I dial the number on the back of it. A woman's voice answers.

"Ranger Information, Jessica speaking. How can I help you?"

I swallow hard and do my best to disguise my voice, speaking low and gravelly. "Someone's going into the woods. They're heading for the old mines. You should send a ranger before they get hurt."

"Miss? What do you mean? Who's going to the mines?"

Crap. She knows I'm a girl. "Just send help. Rangers, cops, whatever." Before Jessica can ask me any more questions, I hang up and toss my phone back in the car. I won't need it where I'm going. No one has ever escaped this thing with a phone call.

As an afterthought, I dig in the glovebox until I find the emergency flashlight I keep there. It's big and heavy, one of those things you could knock someone out with if you bean them with it hard enough. A quick check verifies that the batteries still work. There. Light for the mines, and the added bonus of an extra bludgeoning weapon in case of emergency.

Despite the sudden chill in the air, I'm sweating. My hair is plastered to the back of my neck, the damp curls sticking to my skin. I look like a contestant in a wet t-shirt contest, or maybe a drowned rat. Either way, I'm not winning any beauty pageants with this.

My sweaty fingers slip on the knife handle in my pocket. I try to get a better grip, but it keeps sliding around. How am I supposed to kill the monster when I can't even grab hold of the damn thing?

Each step towards the tree line feels like I'm wearing lead weights on my ankles. The effort is exhausting. At this rate, I'll be too tired to fight the beast when I find it.

The thick fog makes it difficult to see more than a few feet in any direction. All I can see around me are tree trunks and mist. So prevalent is the fog that when I pull the map out of my hoodie pocket, the paper is soggy. I try to unfold it to get my bearings and end up tearing part of it. Right through the site where Cass's body was found. I shiver again at the coincidence and take my time unfolding the rest, not wanting to jinx anything by tearing through an active campsite or something. I'm not overly superstitious, but I just have a bad feeling about, well, everything.

I'm heading to the potential lair of a monster. A beast, a demon, something that's made up of rage and concentrated evil. People have gone after it with guns and been slaughtered all the same. And here I am, carrying only a knife and an iPod. A busted iPod at that! I don't know why I even brought it, except out of habit. I bring it everywhere, and it seemed important to grab it when I got out of the car.

"Well, Cass, here we go. We're really doing this, aren't we?" My voice is small and shaky as I talk to the mist around me. "Gonna go save this kid we don't even know. Save maybe the world. I don't know."

Of course, there's no response. The iPod stays silent and broken.

"Yeah, I know. It's a dumb idea. Can't back out now, though; I gotta follow through. Probably for the first fucking time in my life."

Again, Cass doesn't answer. I figure maybe she's mad at me for running off to get killed. That's fine. Maybe she doesn't know there's a kid's life at stake, or maybe she's being selfish and wanting me to stay alive. Or maybe the iPod is just broken beyond her supernatural ability to make it play. Maybe I should have brought my phone instead. One of those old-school boomboxes from the nineties. Something.

My lips turn up in a nervous grin as I imagine myself lugging one of those beasts on my shoulder, the latest Bone Thugs N Harmony blasting out of the speakers, and I chuckle.

When a low, raspy chuckle answers, I freeze.

Shit. It heard me. It knows I'm here.

With the fog all around me, I can't see it. I can't tell how close it might be, or how far. I listen for any other sounds, like maybe a child crying, but I hear nothing. No birds, no crickets, no leaves rustling in the wind ... It's dead silent.

Shaking off my terror, I square my shoulders and look at the soggy map again. I'm terrible at reading distances on these things, but I figure if I head in the right direction, I'll eventually get there. Just aim for the forbidden zone. What could go wrong?

Okay, I could be murdered. That could go wrong. But what else? I mean, if I prepare for that eventuality, then I guess I'm ready for the worst of it. Right?

Dear God, I hope I'm ready for it.

Images of Kyle's body scroll through my mind as I creep through the woods. There's a tingling feeling in my back, the feeling of being watched. Stalked. Followed.

Followed by whatever got Kyle.

I try to remind myself that this thing has a little kid now. The stakes are higher;

it's not just teenagers and drunk idiots that it's after. It's got a toddler. A *child*. This poor kid hasn't even had a chance at life. That little grinning dude in Two-Feathers' photos needs a chance. A chance to grow up, to live a little.

God, why do I have to have a conscience? If I didn't, I could run away from all this.

Each snap of a twig that I step on echoes in the eerie quiet of the woods. I sound like an elephant tramping through a lumberyard. If the monster wasn't ready for me before, it'll have plenty of chance to be now. Just listen for the pachyderm stomping through the brush.

I stop to double check my direction. The sound of my footsteps halts, and I'm plunged into silence again.

Until another twig snaps.

Shit. How close was that? It's impossible to tell in the thick fog. I think the mist is even affecting the sound, making things echo that shouldn't and muffling other noises. Even if I could hear the monster coming, I'd never be able to tell where it was coming from or how much time I might have to run. I'm screwed.

Blind panic is not a good feeling. It's not particularly helpful in this situation, so I try to tamp it down, but it's no good. My heart is racing, and I'm both freezing and drenched with sweat.

I should have brought a watch. I have no idea how long I've been trudging through Hunting Woods. It could be an hour, could be three. Who knows?

When I finally reach the first of the warning signs declaring the caves off-limits, I stop for a breather. Well, more like a hyperventilator. I can't fucking breathe, and at the same time I can't stop panting. I swallow past a hard lump in my throat and step over the caution tape.

That last step must have been the wrong one—or maybe the right one—because as soon as I'm on the other side, a low growl rumbles somewhere nearby.

It knows I'm here. And it's pissed.

Chapter 16

The passage is narrow, and my flashlight barely cuts through the darkness of the tunnel. I let my hand slide across the rocky surface of the walls. It feels slimy. I shine the light on my hand, and there's a light brown substance left on my fingers. I sniff it and immediately gag. It's the scent of death. I quickly try to wipe the dampness off on my pant leg, but my fingers are still sticky from whatever it is that's coating the walls.

I feel like I'm walking downhill. If it wasn't so cold, I would think I was heading down a steep narrow path to Hell. That could still be the case. Some people's Hell could be ice cold. Who really knows what to expect when they reach the other side? That's what scares everyone the most about dying, right? The whole not knowing what they are in for. I wonder if Cassie will be waiting for me on the other side.

I shiver, knowing I'm heading into some shit but hoping I can complete the mission at hand. If I fail, this thing will be left to kill for many more years to come.

I stop dead in my tracks when I hear a faint cry in the distance. I try to shine the light further down the tunnel, like it will miraculously become brighter, and I'll be able to see something more. I stand as still as possible and turn my head so my ear points in the direction the noise came from, listening.

Nothing.

Am I losing my mind here in the darkness? Is my mind playing tricks on me? I continue to wait for something. Some kind of sound. As I give up and start to walk on, the sound comes again. A faint cry in the distance. It sounds like a child, followed by the clanking of chains.

"Hello?" My voice sounds shaky. "Is anybody there?"

Silence.

I give up and head down the tunnel, trying to clear my mind of everything so I can focus on the task I'm here for. Save the kid; stop the monster.

"Save the kid; stop the monster. Save the kid; stop the monster." I repeat this over and over to myself as I try to keep my breathing steady. The deeper I go into this place, the more scared I get. I feel a weight on my chest, like the world is sitting on top of me, and I have to struggle to get air.

A sobbing sound catches my attention, and I see a flicker of light up ahead of me. I slow down, fear gripping me. I know what's coming, and I'm trying to delay it. There's a bend in the pathway, and I edge closer to it. I peek around the corner and see a huge opening with a fire burning in the middle of the room. Why would the monster need a fire? It's weird and more than a little suspicious.

I spot a small boy by the far wall of the room, cowering down. I hear his sobs, and my heart breaks for him. I recognize him as Two-Feather's grandson.

"Are you ok?" I whisper as I move toward him, checking every corner of the room. He lifts his head, and tears streak his face. "Come on, I'm going to take you home." I reach my hand out to him.

As he moves to take my hand, a shadow passes before my eyes, and the child in front of me transforms into a dark gangly figure, its fingers long and slender, with claws like daggers. It looks up at me and grins. The teeth behind the smile drip saliva.

The monster. It was a trap.

Before I can even think, I'm on my back, and this thing is on top of me. It pokes my chest with its clawed hand. For a moment, everything goes silent. My head is swimming in thoughts, and my vision blurs. Then a ringing starts in my ears, and I hear music start playing from the destroyed iPod, a song I've never heard before.

> *A song, a song, a song will sound*
> *When the Beast comes around*
> *A song not sung, a song profound*
> *A song to make the demon bound*

"I don't fucking understand, Cassie," I find myself screaming. "I need you. Stop playing fucking music and just talk to me." My eyes burn with tears, and the beast digs its claws deeper into my chest. A dampness accumulates on my hoodie, and I look down to see blood gushing from the newly inflicted wound. "Just help me."

"The knife. Use the knife." A whisper in my ear, faint, distant. It's Cassie's voice.

I feel a pressure in my chest, and the thing inserts another claw into me. I gasp for breath and feel myself fading out. I reach my hand down into my pocket and pull out the knife that Kyle gave me.

I have no strength left in me, but I force the knife up and into the monster's chest.

Nothing happens.

The beast's jaw gapes in a grotesque grin, and hot saliva splashes on my cheek.

"You don't even know what to do with that thing," it hisses. "I will eat your soul, and then I'll eat the boy. I'll eat my fill, and you will die knowing you failed."

My head lolls to the side, and I see a small body crumpled in the corner. The thing still has Two-Feather's grandson. It tricked me, but he's still there. His chest rises and falls as he takes a rattling breath, and I know there's a chance, however small, that I can still save him.

"Cassie ..." My vision fades in and out, and I don't even know if I'm saying her name out loud. "Help me."

Her voice whispers to me again. "You're the song, Kit. You have to release the song to stop it."

"I don't understand ..."

"Release the song ..." Cassie's voice fades away, overshadowed by the monster's laughter.

"So delicious," it growls as its tongue

drags across my cheek.

A strange sort of calm flows through me, and I shift my grip on the hilt. It feels like someone else is guiding my hand. With all the strength I have left, I yank the knife out of the beast and turn the blade to face me. I plunge the tip into my chest, crying out in pain as it rips through me. A bright light lances from the stab wound, piercing the monster in the hole I'd left in it.

I thought I'd seen everything in this crazy trip—*heard* everything. Somehow, though, the light surprises me by having a sound to it, a melody, like I just literally released a song from inside me.

The monster's head jerks back, and a howl comes out of its mouth. Slobber splatters across my face from its jowls, and it rips its hand back from my chest. Its body starts to shake as its arms grab at the hole, and a small bubble escapes its chest. The glowing bubble floats above us and starts to form a shape. It morphs into a human form, and I see Cassie. She smiles at me, and I feel almost at peace.

Another orb floats from the hole, and another, one by one, each shifting into a humanoid shape before floating away. Only Cassie's shape remains.

It continues, small balls of light floating out and changing, until the creature collapses on the ground next to me, its body deflated and withered. The sound of shouts and footsteps makes its way to my ears, and I find enough energy to turn my head towards the mouth of the cave. Flashlights. Jessica got help. Two-Feathers' grandson will be okay.

Cassie laughs and floats over me, reaching out her hand. I smile up at her and take her ghostly hand in my pale fingers, and things start to go dark.

"C'mon, sis," her apparition mutters with a heavenly smile. "You did it. Time to rest."

"Will the kid be okay?" My voice wheezes out of me.

"He'll be fine, Kit. You won. Now let's go rest."

"Rest ..." I don't know how I can be any more rested than I am now. My every muscle relaxes, and every nerve releases me from the vice grip of fear I've been living in these past weeks. I'm calm. Detached.

As Cass pulls me higher, I realize just how detached I am. I look down at my body, still hemorrhaging musical light, and a sensation of peace washes over me.

I did it. I ended the soul eater's reign of terror.

<The End>

About the Authors

Angelique Jordonna: Angelique is an author of darkly intense horror, thrillers, and paranormal romance. Her books take you into the depths of depravity while still having elements of the strong love bonds between characters. The rich descriptions pull you right into the story, whether she's detailing a gruesome murder or dropping subtle hints at a burgeoning romance.

Angelique has a love for all things creative, and she devours books and music like they were the finest cuisine, sustaining her better than the finest wines, better than a five-star meal, better than ... sex? Well, maybe not *that* good.

AJ Mullican: AJ is a *USA Today* best-selling author of multiple genres, with a main focus on paranormal romance and dystopian sci-fi. A true indie author, AJ attacks publishing with a DIY attitude and determination.

When not writing or toiling away at her day job in the medical field, AJ can be found exploring the past in the Society for Creative Anachronism. She enjoys making historical garb and practicing her skill at hand embroidery while researching ancient arts. Her home is filled with the pitter-patter of little feet — cat feet, that is. Her two Maine coon mix rescues, Rory and River, keep her company as she writes and sews, while her husband cooks delicious meals.

CPSIA information can be obtained
at www.ICGtesting.com
Printed in the USA
LVHW050820140323
741569LV00009B/580

9 798378 496990